HOLDING HIS HOSTAGE

AMY GAMET

1

———

ill death do us part, you son of a bitch.

Joanne Regan shivered in the bitter December wind as a preacher she'd never met stood over her husband's casket and spoke of God's unending love. David hadn't believed in God. For that reason alone, she'd been sure to get a preacher.

Fiona's mittened hand was clenched tightly in her own, the bitter wind stinging Joanne's bare skin. Her younger daughter had been physically attached to her since learning of David's death—a fist knotted in Jo's hair, a leg crooked over hers on the sofa—as if the connection could keep death from taking her mother, too.

Lucas stood beside Fiona, his yellow ski jacket standing out from the crowd like a daffodil in a pile of ash, and Jo let her gaze rake over the impossibly tall form of her middle child. It was as if he'd simply been stretched, the toddler she remembered pulled into a boy, and she ached to rake her fingers through his wispy blond hair, but he would only pull away if she touched him.

So much pain.

Her throat clenched with an intensity of emotion David's death had failed to stir. Lucas was only beginning to see his father's shortcomings before the anger and resentment had been washed away, a single phone call obliterating all.

She squeezed her eyes shut, her teeth chattering against the cold.

Life without David had long been her dream, but she hadn't wanted him to die, for God's sake. A divorce, neat and clean, the end to this year-long separation and its own new beginning. But he'd fought her at every turn, the bitterness that had grown between them manifesting in custody arrangements and the division of the household.

It had been hardest on April, the oldest of the three at nearly twelve. Joanne turned her head to take in the girl's silhouette, April as still and willowy as a straight pin balanced on end. She was enveloped in one of Joanne's long coats, her hair hanging in thick brown plaits and secured with pink barrettes that surely had been borrowed from Fiona.

April was smack between woman and child, the distance between mother and daughter growing wider by the moment. Just this morning, they'd fought.

Joanne had lifted heavy arms to stir milk into her coffee, cold winter sunshine landing in strips across the table as she contemplated the funeral ahead. April's phone was there, and she picked it up, desperately wanting some insight into the girl's current state of mind.

April was the only one who hadn't cried when Jo told them of their father's death, whether for lack of grief or the inability to express it, Joanne could only guess, having long since been excluded from her daughter's list of confidantes.

Her friends will help her through this, even if she won't confide in me.

God, she hoped that was true, the bold colors and bright photos of Instagram flying by on the screen. She found April's page, but there was no post announcing her father's death, no heart emojis or prayer hands offering solace in her daughter's time of need. She checked the private messages.

I WANT TO MEET YOU.

The words jumped out at her from the screen. She scrolled up to see the earlier conversation, skimming snippets as she went.

You're so funny...

...I love our talks...

My mom is pissing me off...

My dad died.

There it was. Three words in a private message to Justin971, the only evidence of a real friend in a sea of selfies and memes. She frowned, trying to conjure a Justin from her memory of field days and volleyball games, but failing to find a match. She didn't even know who April's friends were anymore, and the knowledge hurt her heart.

"What do you think you're doing?"

She'd never seen April so angry.

Fiona tugged on her hand, pulling her back to the present. "I gotta go potty," she whispered.

"Just a few more minutes. Can you wait?"

The girl stuck out her bottom lip but nodded. "I'm cold."

"I know. Me, too."

Jo turned back to the preacher, the familiar lines of the psalm washing over her, constricting her throat. They'd been happy together once, hadn't they? It had been so many years, she could barely remember if it was true. The lies were far more easily brought to mind, the betrayal, the pain, the verbal abuse.

The wind kicked up and she squinted against it, her eyes

coming to rest on the deep brown casket as she visualized what must be inside. Poor David. No one deserved to die as he had. The funeral director had asked if she wanted to see the remains, but she couldn't bear the idea. Just how much of him was left after the fire?

She looked around for the plainclothes police detective who'd been standing near the hearse when they arrived. He must have seen the body, read the coroner's report. Maybe she should ask him. Bump herself up the list of suspects with one fell swoop. But instead of the detective, her stare collided with the green and bloodshot eyes of David's mistress. Jo's stomach bottomed out as if she'd swallowed battery acid.

McKenzie Bannon stood with her arm tucked into the crook of her husband's, her wavy red hair falling gracefully over her shoulders. If Richard Bannon knew about the affair, he gave no indication. He was one of the most prominent clients of David's firm, that connection being the primary reason McKenzie had gotten the job as David's secretary all those years ago.

If you thought about it, Richard Bannon was the reason Jo's entire life had fallen apart. There she went again, making excuses for David, putting the blame at someone else's feet instead of his, where it rightfully belonged. Bannon hadn't made her husband cheat on her.

"I'm sorry for your loss, Mrs. Regan," said a man's voice behind her, startling her. The service had ended. She vaguely recognized the pudgy, balding man as an accountant from David's firm.

"We were separated," she blurted, unsure why she needed to offer that information right now. "A year in February."

"I hadn't heard." He mumbled an awkward goodbye,

another balding accountant stepping in to take his place. This time, she kept her marital status to herself. From the corner of her eye, she saw April approach the casket while Lucas wandered among the headstones nearby.

"I gotta go potty," repeated Fiona, tugging on her arm.

"Go tell your brother it's time to leave." She addressed the line of mourners waiting to pay their respects, grateful at least McKenzie hadn't set foot in that line. "I'm sorry, I need to go." She turned abruptly and crossed to April, bracing herself for the girl's potential attitude. "You doing okay?" Jo asked.

"When will they lower the casket into the ground?"

"After we leave, I suppose."

"I want them to do it now."

"Why?"

April didn't answer. Suddenly even colder than she had been, Jo wrapped her arms around her midsection. "Come on. Fiona's gotta go potty." April reluctantly fell into step beside her, Lucas and Fiona joining them as they headed for the car, the unwavering stare of the police detective tracking them like the moon on a cloudless night.

She wanted to tell him she hadn't killed her husband. If she was going to do that, she'd have done it long before now. The service was done. David would soon be in the ground, and she'd played the part of the dutiful wife for the very last time, albeit not terribly well.

"Mrs. Regan?"

She bristled at the name, turning to see Richard Bannon hustling to catch up to her, and she stifled a suffering sigh. "Yes?"

"I'm sorry for your loss."

"Thank you." She moved to turn around, knowing she was being rude but no longer caring. She needed to get out of this place, anxious to get to her vehicle and find Fiona a bathroom, but he grabbed her upper arm.

"Can I have a word with you? It'll just take a second."

She jerked her arm out of his grasp, irritated with his touch and considering telling him so. But it was a difficult day, and the easiest path was the one of least resistance. "Go on to the car," she told the kids. "I'll be right there."

When they were gone, he said, "Beautiful family."

"Thank you." She took a shaking breath in. "I only have a minute. My daughter needs to use the bathroom."

"We always wanted kids, McKenzie and me. Such a blessing." He put his hands in his pockets. "You know I did business with your husband. A lot of business over the years."

She shifted her weight. "Of course. The firm has many excellent accountants who can help you. I'm sure they'll work to make the transition—"

"I don't want to seem indelicate on the day you're burying your husband, but I have a problem. David was in possession of a great deal of money at the time of his death. My money."

She took a step back. "I don't know anything about David's business dealings. We were separated." *Because he was fucking your wife.* "If you'll excuse me."

His hand shot out again, strong fingers locking painfully around her upper arm.

"Let go of me!" She yanked her arm, but he kept his hold.

"Money that needs to be returned."

Her eyes shot to the spot where the police detective had been standing, but he'd walked to the winding cemetery road and was getting into an SUV. There were no mourners left, Bannon and Joanne the last ones around, and she wondered where McKenzie had gone. She swallowed against her dry throat. "How much money?"

"Two-point-three million."

She gasped. "I don't have it. I don't know anything about any money."

"He didn't take it with him, which means it's somewhere on this side of the great beyond. I need your help to find it."

"You don't understand. We were getting a divorce. He didn't share money with me. We didn't share anything."

"Except your children." He turned her so she faced the vehicle. "Look at them. It would be such a shame if anything happened to one of them."

A trickle of fear ran down her spine. "Are you threatening me?" His clawlike fingers dug into her flesh. April stared back at her with wide, worried eyes, the yellow of Lucas's coat just barely visible behind her.

"I prefer to think of it as motivating you to do the right thing."

"You wouldn't hurt them," she whispered.

"Like I didn't hurt your husband?"

Her mouth fell open, her stare fixed on the dilated pupils of his eyes, wolflike and predatory. Was this the last thing David had seen? This monster of a man bearing down on him, demanding money? David had been shot, his body burned beyond recognition as his hunting cabin went up in flames around him.

If Bannon killed David, he was capable of terrible things. The vision changed, Bannon now holding young Lucas in his clutches, and her heart skipped a beat as terror flooded her nervous system.

"You have one week, Joanne." He lowered his voice. "You get me my money, or the oldest one dies."

The detective's SUV rounded the corner, heading toward

them. Bannon looked from her to the vehicle and back again and growled, "You go to the police or the feds, and I'll kill all three. You got that?"

He released her. She watched helplessly as the detective passed her minivan and drove away.

"We'll be watching you, Mrs. Regan. Now go find my money."

2

____

Joanne gripped the steering wheel tightly, the slick snow-covered roadway glowing in the dim light of dusk as they got close to home. Her skin prickled, dry air from the heating vent blowing in her face, and she was sure she would never be warm ever again.

Lucas and April bickered, but she wasn't listening. Fear was a funny thing. It had the power to immobilize you, or to force the weakest muscles into profound action worthy of an Olympic athlete. She was waiting to see which reaction would prevail.

She'd grown up in a house of fear, never knowing what the day would bring. Times like these, when fear tucked itself tightly between her collarbone and heart, she relied on her upbringing to fuel her race to safety.

But this was different. How the hell was she going to find that money? For nearly four hundred days, she'd been painstakingly untangling her life from David's, a slow and difficult process that couldn't be undone.

"Who was that man?" asked April.

"Someone your dad worked with."

"He grabbed your arm."

"He was upset."

"Why?"

"Who knows why people do things, April? It's a difficult time for us all." She drove by the police station, wishing she could walk inside and find safety, but she knew in her heart all safety was gone.

"I think he's following us."

Their eyes met. Joanne adjusted the rearview mirror. She hadn't been paying attention, and she cursed herself. "Are you sure?"

"Yes."

She turned onto a two-lane road that led to her property outside of town and sped up, watching as the car behind her followed suit. Her hands broke out in a sweat. "Just the man, or the woman, too?"

"I don't know."

I'll be watching you.

This man had killed David; now he was after her. She needed help, her mind desperately searching for anyone she could turn to and coming up empty. Perhaps the police could protect them, but would they even believe her? That detective seemed to think she was a murderer. That definitely wasn't a chance she could take.

Jo turned onto their street, her hands gripping the steering wheel so hard it was difficult to move the wheel. She couldn't catch her breath, the anxiety that was her constant companion now spiraling into a full-fledged panic attack. They needed to get away, to find somewhere safe. She needed to protect her family.

But how?

The house appeared in the distance, a white rail fence and acres of manicured rolling hills surrounding a big white ranch with a barn and stable visible in the distance. She suddenly wished that fence were electrified and at least twenty feet high, but even as she thought it, she knew she still wouldn't feel safe with that man somewhere out there.

She pulled to the side of the road and stopped at her mailbox, April putting her window down and collecting the mail. Behind them, the car had stopped some hundred feet back, headlights blazing. They weren't even trying to be inconspicuous. This was an intimidation game, a tactic to terrorize her, and it was working.

She pulled into the drive, fresh snow crunching under her tires. She waited to see if the other car would follow.

"Who's Evelyn Nowak?" asked April.

"Evelyn?" The name was a relic from her past, a part of her life that seemed more like a story about someone else than an actual piece of her memory. But if that was true, then Evelyn was one of the best parts of the book. "An old friend. My ex-boyfriend's mother. Probably a sympathy card."

"Looks like it."

Jo glanced in the rearview. The car stayed on the main road with its lights on. Better than following them to the door, but worse than driving away.

"How old were you?" April asked.

"Seventeen." She opened the garage door and pulled inside. Her panic was subsiding, and she knew it was the mention of Evelyn's name that had comforted her so quickly. There was only one place she'd ever really felt secure, only one place she'd ever had a friend she could trust and people who felt like family. That was in Evelyn's house, and she longed to be back there now.

She pushed the ridiculous idea out of her mind. To get there, she would need to cross a bridge she had long since burned to the ground. She would feel better when she got inside and set the alarm. Make herself a cup of tea and get some perspective on this whole god-awful day. Maybe try to log in to David's bank account and see just how much money he had squirreled away.

She grabbed the mail and her purse, her finger trailing over Evelyn's perfectly formed script as the kids climbed out of the car.

"I get the Xbox," called Lucas, racing ahead.

"I want princesses!" whined Fiona, trailing after him.

April got out but turned back. "You coming?"

"I'll be right in." The door closed, the car suddenly filled with silence. She took a deep breath and opened the envelope. A watercolor iris graced the front of the card, and she knew immediately Evelyn had painted it by hand. Inside, she read, "Dearest Joanne, I was so sad—"

The garage door to the kitchen opened and Lucas appeared, screaming, "*Mom!*"

She held up a finger, continuing to read. "—to learn of David's passing. I wish I were there, so I could give you my shoulder on which to cry. When you're ready, please come for a visit so I can hug you properly and reminisce. Love always—"

A knock at her window made her jump. April stood on the other side. "You need to come see this."

The horrified tone had her scrambling to get inside. Something was clearly wrong. Had Fiona hurt herself? She pushed the door open and froze.

Utter destruction.

Drawers from the antique hutch were strewn about the floor, their contents scattered about like leaves in the fall. Pictures had been taken off walls, their frames and canvases separated with slices and rips.

She stumbled toward the kitchen, Lucas weaving his way through the room like he was crossing a pond on stones. "Who would do this?" he asked.

"I don't know," Jo lied, avoiding April's knowing stare as she bent and picked up a picture of the kids, its glass shattered and wooden frame fractured. It was a favorite of hers, their last family portrait, and she pushed the glass aside, cutting her finger. She gasped and popped it in her mouth.

A sudden shriek echoed through the house. The picture forgotten, Jo flew down the hallway toward Fiona's screams. She should have grabbed a knife from a kitchen drawer, and she chastised herself as she ran, rounding the corner to Fiona's room.

The little girl stood in the middle of the space, surrounded by toys and clothes and discarded drawers, wailing. "Somebody hurt my dolly!" She held out her favorite doll, and Joanne felt the blood drain out of her head. The doll's face had been cut open in one long line from her eye to her chin.

An image of Evelyn's house stood out in her mind like a lighthouse in a stormy sea. The epitome of safety. Someone who could help. Did Sloan still live in town? She didn't know how she would handle it if he did, but her discomfiture over seeing her old boyfriend was truly trivial right now.

April and Lucas appeared in the door. "Get your things," said Jo, her voice a choked rasp. "Pack a bag. Underwear. Socks. Shirts. Pants." No one moved. Fiona kept crying, and Jo picked her up, despite how heavy the girl had gotten.

"Where are we going?" asked Lucas.

It was the only possible place, just that single destination, no matter how long it had been since she'd been there or all the reasons she left. "My hometown."

"You have a hometown?"

"He'll follow us," said April.

Lucas looked from one to the other, clearly not following but not asking, either.

"Not if they don't know we've left." Joanne's plan clicked firmly into place. "We'll take the Porsche. We'll drive out by the stables and avoid the main road."

Fiona jerked her head back to look at her mother. "Daddy wouldn't like that."

"I'm sure he wouldn't mind." Jo wiped a tear from Fiona's cheek. David moved out a year ago, but his apartment didn't have a garage in which to store his most prized possession.

Lucas rolled his eyes. "Oh, yes, he would!"

She took a trembling breath in, terrified of what lay ahead. "We'll go as soon as it's dark." She put Fiona down and kissed her head. "Come on. We all need to pack our things. It's a long drive from Chicago to New York."

3

———————

Sloan Dvorak had two pair, aces over fives. From the grumpy-ass look on Mac's lined brown face, Sloan would bet his boss had a whole lot of nothing. Picking up the largest Funyun from the bowl, Sloan put it in his mouth and crushed it loudly with his teeth.

"Close your damn mouth," barked Mac, clucking his tongue. "Got no fucking manners at all, like you were raised by goddamn wolves."

Actually, he'd been raised right in this very house, though his father had long since passed away and his mother was retired and off seeing the world. That made the old family home more or less Sloan's, and poker games with the guys were one of his favorite ways to fill it.

Sloan smiled through a mouthful of Funyuns. Mac definitely didn't have anything. "I love your soft, sensitive side. You in?"

"I'll raise you ten."

Sloan turned to Moto, HERO Force's resident computer genius. "What about you? You want to give me more of your money, or are you saving up for more hair gel?" Moto's sleek black hair streaked backward from a widow's peak, an endless source of entertainment for the team.

"You wish you had hair like this." Moto laid down his cards. "But I fold."

Sloan picked up another Funyun and gestured to his own head. "The women dig the sloppy curly look. They think it's sexy."

Mac grunted. "You look like a cocker spaniel."

Sloan nodded. "But a very sexy cocker spaniel who can cook." He tossed a Funyun to his old dog, Gus. As if to prove his last point, he stood and went to the oven, pulling out a tray of filet mignon and Brie hors d'oeuvres that smelled like heaven, dusting them with finishing salt.

"I wouldn't date either one of you motherfuckers." Trace Langston's voice was deep and raspy, his heavy drawl testament to his southern roots. "Grab me a beer while you're up."

Sloan grabbed a bottle and the snacks, setting both on the barnwood table. "You in?"

Trace threw a handful of poker chips into the pot and reached for the beer. "I hate this game. Where are Gavin and Asher tonight? At least I can take their money."

"Honduras," said Mac. "Give me three." He discarded and Sloan dealt him more cards. "They ran into some trouble with the government. Lying low for a couple days until the embassy can get them out."

Sloan looked to Trace with raised eyebrows.

"None for me," said Trace.

"None? Shit. Dealer takes one." Sloan put down the six of hearts and picked up another ace. "What about Champion?"

"He had a date." Mac sighed heavily and put his cards

face down. "I fold. Pass that over here." He gestured to the food.

Sloan turned to Trace. "Guess it's just you and me, Langston."

Mac moaned. "Damn, that's good."

"Try it with the Funyuns." Sloan passed the bowl down.

"I'll raise you forty." Trace rubbed his beard.

Sloan smiled. "I call."

"Sweet mother of God," said Mac, pointing to the plate. "When I'm on my deathbed, I want you to make me that. You can just shove it in my mouth until it blocks my airway."

Trace turned over his cards. "Flush."

"You dick." Sloan turned over his full house.

Trace smiled and winked before raking the chips toward himself. "Always a pleasure doing business with ya, Dvorak."

Moto lifted his chin toward Trace. "We should get going."

"I'm just getting warmed up," Trace whined.

Moto stood. "Your designated driver has to be on a plane for Wyoming at five in the morning."

"So do I. We can sleep on the way. It's a four-hour flight."

Sloan leaned back in his chair. Moto was the epitome of discipline, managing to squeeze more into a day than most people did in a week. There was no way in hell Trace would convince him to go off schedule. "Thanks for coming by," said Sloan.

Trace reluctantly stood and burped. "When you go wheels up, Dvorak?"

"Got a few days off." He walked Trace and Moto to the door and said his goodbyes. He made himself a gin and tonic before joining Mac back at the table. It was time for them to have a conversation, one he'd been dreading for months. But first, he needed to check on his friend. "You look tired, old man."

"I feel it."

"Any news on Ellie?" Mac's wife had left him years earlier, and every moment he wasn't doing official HERO Force business, Mac was looking for her.

Sloan was aware of Mac's stare fixing on the gin and tonic. Mac didn't drink, but Sloan had long suspected it was because he might never stop if he did. The man had a hunger about him that never seemed to be satisfied. Men like that often chose to be numb rather than constantly chase fulfillment.

"Waiting on the DNA results from the bodies we found down south. Making me goddamn stir-crazy."

"I'm praying for good news for you, man."

Mac grunted. "Sometimes I wonder what the hell that would be. I hope she's alive, of course. But if she is, she doesn't want me in her life. I don't see a happy ending in sight."

Sloan didn't believe that was completely true. If Mac wasn't holding out hope, there would be no point in searching for his wife. On the contrary, searching for Ellie seemed to be the only constant Mac really had. "People can surprise you. Even somebody you've completely given up on can turn around and make good. Be part of your life again. You just fight the good fight until you find her."

"Oh, I ain't giving up. Just think I'm out of my damn mind, is all." He reached for another filet mignon snack. You ever been married, Dvorak?"

"Came close once, but I dodged that bullet."

"Somebody told me once, even people you've given up on can come back and make good."

Sloan laughed. "Not this time."

"So, what's going on with you? You been looking like Atlas, carrying the weight of the world on your shoulders and shit."

"Noticed that, huh?" He took a sip of his drink and shrugged. This talk was long overdue, but that didn't make it any easier. "How do I put this? I'm thinking maybe this business isn't for me, after all."

"HERO Force?"

"Yeah."

"Why's that?"

"People are counting on me. There's a reason you can't be a Navy SEAL with one arm, Mac."

"Once a SEAL, always a SEAL."

"You know what I mean." He swirled his glass, a bright green lime wedge moving in circles. "A man needs two arms and two legs to be a good soldier."

"You're preaching to the choir on that one, boy."

"You barely even limp. I'm missing my whole arm."

"I can't run worth a damn, and we both gotta strap on a limb to make ourselves whole. What's this about, Sloan? You feeling sorry for yourself all of a sudden?"

"Mexico." He leaned back in his chair. He'd been on a HERO Force mission when the shit hit the fan. "My prosthetic can't keep up with the real thing. I lost my grip on my weapon, missed a shot that nearly got Razorback killed."

"He didn't mention it."

"He didn't know." He looked at his hands on either side of his glass, one flesh and bone, one resin and metal.

Mac sighed and leaned forward in his chair. "You're a highly trained soldier. One of the elite."

He blew out air. "I'm a fucking liability."

"Bullshit. You go looking for reasons, you can find one

every man on my team doesn't belong there. But you stop looking, and all you see are good, strong, capable men."

"Is that good enough? We're protecting lives every day out there, shooting firearms that could blast a hole through a man in a fraction of a second, then do it again."

"What are you saying? You want out?"

Sloan cocked his head. "Yeah, man. I am."

"No."

"Come on. You know I've got a point. You know I'm telling you the truth when I say we came this close to losing that battle down in Mexico, and it would have been my goddamn fault. Me, Razorback, Jackie, her kid... all of us would have been dead."

"Listen to me, kid. You take what you're given in life and you make the best of it that you can. Are you the same soldier you were when you worked for Uncle Sam? Hell no. You're wiser. You're smarter. You're seasoned, for God's sake."

Sloan laughed without humor. "Seasoned. I'm a fucking gimp."

"So what? You gonna lock yourself up in your mama's house and bake for the rest of your life? You have a gift. You have a responsibility to use it for the greater good, Dvorak."

"Yeah, well, I think the greater good would be better served if I retired."

There was a knock at the door, and Gus launched himself toward it, barking. One of the guys must have forgotten something. The old husky never appeared younger than when he was defending his turf, his bark sounding far more fierce than he'd actually been in years.

"All right, boy, calm down." He rounded the corner toward the front door just as Gus stopped barking, his ferocity replaced by excited dancing and an eager whine. Sloan cocked his head. The dog would never react that way for the HERO Force guys. Was his mother back early from her trip? Why hadn't she called him for a ride home from the airport?

He approached the door, the melodic sounds of a woman's voice audible through the thick wood panels, and froze. That wasn't his mother's voice, though it was one he knew well. He stared at the dog for a long beat, watching him jump and dance as he listened to the woman.

It couldn't be.

The doorbell rang a second time and he stood rooted to the spot as the dog went crazy. "Okay, okay," he whispered to the animal. "Calm down." Taking a deep breath, he opened the door, and just as Gus had indicated, there stood the woman who'd broken his heart.

4
____

"*All right, boy, calm down.*"

Joanne's eyes went wide. She stood on the porch of the old Victorian house, suddenly wishing the boards would open beneath her feet and swallow her deep into the earth. Anyplace would be better than here, any moment far better than this one. That wasn't Evelyn, that sounded like Sloan!

She looked longingly back at the Porsche idling in the driveway, a big plume of exhaust glowing behind it in the light of a streetlamp. She wished she could run back to it and drive far away from this house, this town, and the memories that lived here.

Heavy footsteps approached the door, but it was that voice that lit her anxiety like a fuse. She was positive it was him, and the dog sounded like Gus. She'd been seventeen when she left Hyde Park, the furry white Husky mix just a puppy who liked to sleep between her feet. That was what, thirteen years ago? "Gus, is that you, baby?"

The dog whined and she smiled wide, needing to focus

on the dog instead of the human being on the other side of that door. "Oh, sweetie, I missed you so much!"

The footsteps had stopped, but no one answered the door. She closed her eyes tightly and pressed the doorbell a second time. This time it opened, a rectangle of light from the kitchen door putting the figure in silhouette. Still, she recognized him as she would from any angle, and a visceral ache stabbed her abdomen. "Hi, Sloan," she squeaked.

For long moments, he didn't move or respond. Then the storm door opened and the dog pushed out, jumping up onto her thighs and licking her face. Joanne laughed, petting the animal she'd once considered her own and wiping away his kisses. The light came on over her head and she squinted against it.

"Okay, that's enough, get down," he said.

She straightened and looked back at him. His eyes struck her first, as they always had—an arresting hazel of golden green that was his alone. Thick dark hair settled in waves and curls, and she remembered the feel of it slipping through her fingers as he moved on top of her. He was bulkier now than he had been, more muscular, the change turning what had been boyish good looks into something dangerous and fine. His brow, always heavy and starkly masculine, emphasized the glare he was giving her. She swallowed.

"Jo, what are you doing here?"

"Well, I'm not selling Girl Scout cookies." She snapped her fingers and pointed at him with a smile, the joke garnering no response. She cleared her throat. "I was looking for your mom."

"She's in Machu Pichu."

"Oh..." *Fuck.*

"Come on in." He moved over for her to enter, holding

open the door with one arm. She squeezed between him and the doorframe just as Gus pushed past her legs, knocking her off-balance and directly into his chest. His warm body carried his familiar scent straight to her brain. His arm came around to steady her, and she jerked away from the contact, righting herself and nearly jumping out of his embrace. "Sorry."

"It's okay."

She moved ahead of him to the kitchen, so aware of his presence behind her that her back tingled, and she needed to remind herself how to walk. The smell of something savory hung heavy on the air, and her mouth watered, reminding her she hadn't eaten in hours. He'd always been an excellent cook, and her empty stomach longed for the food that smelled so good.

It struck her at once—here she was, starving and desperate, while his home was warm and full of food and anything she could possibly need. That had always been the dynamic between them, and it pained her to realize not even that had changed.

She entered the kitchen. A dark-skinned man sat at the table, fit and wiry, traces of silver shining in the scruff on his cheeks. "I'm sorry," she said. "I didn't realize you had company."

"Joanne Buckley, Mac O'Brady. Mac, this is Jo." He sat down, gesturing to a chair at a wide barn-wood table.

"I was just about to hit the road." Mac stood.

She put her hand on her chest. "Don't let me chase you out."

"Nah, this fool was talking nonsense anyway. Good time to take my leave." He took a black leather coat off the back of his chair and slipped his arm into the sleeve. "Though I wouldn't mind you putting some of those snacks into a ziplock bag for me, Dvorak."

Joanne took a seat, her stomach growling as she watched Sloan get food for his friend and say goodbye. When he was through, Sloan brought the tray back to the table. "Help yourself."

Her nervous stomach warred briefly with her hunger, and she took one. "Thanks."

"What brings you to town? Is it your father?"

She shook her head. "God, no. I don't even know if he's alive or dead."

"Alive, last I knew."

"Fabulous." She looked at her hands. This was harder than she could have imagined. "I was really hoping to see your mom."

"She'll be back a week from Friday."

Shit.

Her hand trembled, her stomach rioting against the food she'd just swallowed. "That doesn't really help me."

"Anything I can do?"

"Uhm..." She would rather ask the devil himself for a favor, but it's not like that was an option. She bit her lip.

He leaned back. "I haven't seen you in thirteen years, then you show up on my doorstep at one in the morning. Gotta be something."

"I thought your mom would be here. She sent me a card." He furrowed his brow, and she wondered if he knew David was dead. She'd been hoping they could stay here, but now that plan was all shot to hell. She had a little more than two hundred dollars in cash and hadn't thought to use her bank card before she left town. Now she was afraid of leaving a trail. "I need help."

"Name it."

"Money." That was the least of it, but it was certainly a start. Running away with a family of four didn't come cheaply.

"How much?"

"A few thousand." She looked away, eyes stinging as she desperately tried not to cry. What must he think of her?

His chair scraped the wood floor as he stood. "Cash or check?"

"Aren't you going to ask what for?"

"You wouldn't be here unless you need it." He opened a cupboard and returned with a checkbook.

"Cash would be better."

He closed the checkbook and tossed the pen on the table. "I can get it in the morning when the bank opens up."

The movement caused the sleeve of his T-shirt to shift, revealing a line in the middle of his bicep where the color changed by several shades. She stared at it, trying to make sense of what she was seeing.

He lowered his arm and raised his sleeve, revealing the point where a prosthetic arm joined his body. She sucked in air. "What happened?"

"Kandahar. Do you have someplace to stay?"

"My kids are in the car."

The air seemed to shift, the time and experience that separated them now living, breathing forces in the room.

"How old are they?"

"Fiona's four, Lucas is seven, and April's eleven."

"You can stay here. All of you."

She opened her mouth to object but stopped herself. It was a big house, with plenty of room for them all if they shared. The kids would love a clean bed as much as she would, warm blankets and fluffy pillows. She swallowed what was left of her pride. "Thank you." An awkward silence settled between them. "I really appreciate this, Sloan." She stood up. "Fiona's asleep. Where should I put her?"

He stood, too. "Anywhere's up for grabs. I'll take the couch so you can have the bedrooms."

"You don't need to do that."

"Come on, Buckley," he said, using her maiden name. "You look like you've been through the war. It's just a couch." He grinned.

"Thanks for pointing that out." She returned the smile. He'd always had a big heart. She'd nearly forgotten what it was like to be on the receiving end of so much generosity, and she was getting choked up. "I'll just grab the kids."

She hustled out the door and back into the cold, climbing into the driver's seat and turning off the car. "Come on. We're staying here tonight."

Lucas was in the backseat. "This place looks haunted."

"It's not haunted," she said, knowing full well Sloan's mother would probably disagree. "Grab your things." She got out and opened Fiona's door, unbuckling the sleeping girl and picking her up, Jo's back insisting she stop lifting the girl soon.

The four of them stomped up the wooden steps, setting off another round of barking from Gus. "Whose house is this?" asked April.

"An old friend's." Both kids turned to look at her, and she shrugged. "I had friends once." The kids still stared. "It was a long time ago." She huffed. "It's cold out here. Come on, I'll introduce you to the dog."

5

—————

Sloan took a sip of twenty-year-old scotch, the liquid burning a pleasant trail down his throat and into his belly. It was two o'clock in the morning, his high school girlfriend was putting her kids to sleep in his house, and he couldn't help but wonder if he'd wandered into one of those Christmas movies his mom liked to watch.

Any minute now, one of Joanne's kids would come knocking on the study door and call him Daddy, and he'd have the ten days between now and Christmas to see if he'd made the right decision all those years ago by letting Joanne get away.

He'd held his breath when she told him the ages of the children, wondering if fate had dealt him an unexpected wild card, but clearly that wasn't the case. From the look of them, the kids had all been fathered by David Regan, and he ground his teeth just thinking about the other man.

He took another sip of his drink, wondering what had brought her here like this. She needed money, and the desperation he'd seen painted on her features was deeply concerning. It had taken a lot for her to come here—even if it was to see Evelyn and not him—which spoke volumes for her other options. He knew she didn't have family she could turn to, but didn't she have friends? Someone closer than him who could come to the rescue?

Not that he minded the money. He would never begrudge her that. He swirled the liquid in his glass. They'd been in the same class for as long as he could remember. She was the daughter of the meanest man in town, Old Man Buckley, who ran a gas station and smoke shop—a perilous combination forever begging to explode. She'd come to school in dirty clothes with her hair unbrushed, day after day, and kept mostly to herself.

By high school, she'd looked more like the other kids and even had a few friends, but Sloan was observant. He noticed the worn-out seams on her jeans, the sewn-up strap on her purse, the hole in the sole of her sneaker. More important, he noticed the occasional bruise or shiner, and the way she jumped when approached from behind.

He'd been drawn to her, fueled by his need to protect and defend the innocent, and later by the fiercest cravings of his body. She was sweetness and light, with eyes that could see deep into his soul and a touch that could set him on fire.

If he was being honest, their relationship held a kind of intensity he hadn't experienced since. He'd told himself it was because they were young, because she was his first, but as soon as she'd stood in his kitchen tonight, he knew he'd been lying to himself. The intensity was right where he'd left it, invisible at her feet, waiting only for him to pick it up and hang on for the ride.

Only difference was, now he knew where that ride would lead, and it was a road he had no desire to travel again. When she'd left him for Regan, he learned what was really important to her. Financial security. Escaping from this town and her abusive father. A promise in the form of a thin gold band, no matter who had slipped it on her finger.

Joanne had been looking for someone to save her. He had been looking for love. He refilled his drink.

What had happened with her husband? Clearly she and the kids were on their own, but he'd wager money there was more to that story than met the eye, and it wouldn't surprise him if David Regan was somehow responsible for the mess she was in. As far as Sloan was concerned, Regan was an asshole.

He'd moved to town senior year, and Sloan had a bad feeling about that guy from the moment they met. But even if you'd warned him that six months later Regan would be married to Sloan's girl, he never would have believed it.

Betrayal was like that, knocking you down when you least expected it.

Yeah, he would definitely not be picking up with Joanne again, intensity be damned. He'd give her the money she needed, make sure she was okay, and wish her well on her way out the door. Get his goddamn bed back. Wash her scent off his sheets. Hell, maybe he would burn them.

There was a knock on the study door. "Can I come in?" she called.

"Sure."

Her skin glowed in the dim light, her dark hair swept back from her face to reveal the curve of her neck. The sweet scent of soap and shampoo wafted to him on the air. "I hope you don't mind, I took a shower."

Mind that you stripped naked in my house and wrapped yourself in one of my towels? I'll have to burn those, too.

"Not at all."

She passed the couch and settled into a leather club chair closest to him, draping her legs over the armrest, just as she used to do. There was a familiarity to her being here that he found both comforting and ominous, and he wondered if a moth felt this exact sensation while staring into a flame.

"Lucas is asleep, finally. Fiona never woke up. I'm not so sure about April. What are you drinking?"

"Scotch. Want some?"

She nodded and he resisted the urge to pass his glass for her to sip. Instead he rose, taking a clean one from a sideboard and pouring from a crystal decanter that had once been his father's. "Did you have enough blankets?"

"Plenty. Thank you for giving up your bedroom and letting us stay."

"You can stop thanking me now." An image of her snuggled up in his bed appeared unbidden in his mind, stolen moments when she'd snuck in to spend the night with him. His mom had let her all but live in their house, so long as she returned to her own every evening. Little did Evelyn know how rarely that actually happened.

As if reading his mind, Jo asked, "How is your mom these days?"

She'd always been able to do that, seeming to sense exactly what he was thinking when he said nothing at all. Once, it had been endearing, but now, it unnerved him. "She's good. Spends most of her time traveling." He finished his drink and resisted the urge to refill it. "That's her camper in the driveway. "

"I didn't notice."

"You didn't? Thirty-two feet of freedom, she calls it."

She laughed softly. "Good for her. Your mom deserves every bit of happiness."

"She would have loved to have seen you."

"Me, too."

He stared at his empty glass, considering the wisdom of what he was about to say. "Why me, Jo?"

"Excuse me?" Those cool blue eyes connected with his own.

Once, he'd thought she was an open book, but now he knew better. Those eyes that could seem so sincere were capable of hiding her emotions. "You have Illinois plates. You drove all the way here with three kids in tow to borrow money. Why?"

Her cheeks filled with color. "There was no one else I could ask."

"I find that hard to believe."

"Believe what you want." She stood. "I should get some sleep."

"Don't run away from me."

"I'm not running."

He stood and rounded the desk. "You don't want to discuss it, so you're walking away to end the conversation, just like you always do."

She shrugged. "There's nothing to discuss. You want to know why I picked you to beg for money, and I told you. I don't have anyone else."

"Why not?"

"I don't know. How many people could you borrow money from?"

"Lots."

She rolled her eyes. "We're not all as well liked as the infamous Sloan Dvorak."

"You are liked just fine." He was close to her now, her eyes suspiciously glassy, and he suspected if he pushed her she would break, her problems crashing into him like water bursting from a fractured dam. That was a bad idea, but he couldn't help himself any more than he could avoid drowning in the flood. "Talk to me, Buckley. Tell me about your life, if just for old times' sake."

"What do you want me to say?" She gestured with her arms. "That I don't have any friends, that no one would be willing to help me if I lay bleeding in the street?"

"Why is that?"

She shut her eyes. "Just forget it. I'm sorry I said anything."

His hand closed around her upper arm, and she felt good, better than he expected, better than he wanted to deal with. "You're a nice person. What makes you think they wouldn't help you?"

"They don't even know me."

"We all feel that way sometimes."

"No, you don't get it. They don't know me at all, literally. I don't socialize with them. I say no if one of the moms asks me for coffee. I'm not in the PTA. I don't have friends, Sloan."

A tear ran down her face, and he followed its trail to the corner of her mouth. She was one of the most generous people he'd ever known, so full of life and spirit. It didn't make any sense. "Why the hell not?"

"David didn't like it."

He took in her defensive posture, the emotion in her face, and a tingle went up his spine. He'd seen her like this before. The deer-in-the-headlights stare, an energy borne of fear seeming to overtake her presence. She was like this after run-ins with her father, confrontations that were always full of violence whether he hurt her physically or not.

"Did he hurt you?" Adrenaline pumped into his bloodstream, that need to defend rising up from within.

"Of course not," she snapped.

"Then where is he?"

"Just because I don't have my husband with me doesn't mean he abused me. I would never stay with someone like that. You know me better than that."

He sure did, and on more than one occasion, he'd regretted not killing her old man for what he'd put her through. But she seemed to be telling the truth, which meant he was overreacting. He nodded. "Right. I just thought... I'm sorry."

She dropped her arms to her sides. "I'm going to bed." She picked up her drink. "It's been a very long day."

He nodded. "Sleep well." He watched as she padded to the door on bare feet, her hips swaying alluringly. "First thing in the morning, I'll run to the bank."

And you can get out of my life forever.

"Good night, Sloan." She smiled softly and slipped out of his study.

Sloan squeezed the skin between his eyes, and cursed.

6

————

Joanne lay on her back beside Fiona in Sloan's bed, staring at the ceiling. She'd spent two hours on her phone, trying to guess the password to David's bank account without success, before Googling how long it took for a family to receive a dead person's assets. While it might not have been the best source of information, every Reddit user agreed it would take a heck of a lot longer than a week.

That's assuming the money was in his account, which she doubted. She had a hard time imagining straightlaced David stealing a nickel from anyone, but even if he really had taken Bannon's money, such a clandestine act seemed to require greater effort in hiding the proceeds.

With a sigh, she flopped onto her side, but every time she pressed her cheek into the pillow, all she could smell was Sloan.

Fear for her children's safety and her residual feelings for Sloan took turns at the forefront of her mind, neither one of which was helping her sleep, though the latter was highly preferable to ponder than the first.

She pulled back the covers and walked to a wide double window, moonlight illuminating the snowfall and white yard below. With a sigh, she leaned her forehead against the glass. She never would have come here if she knew it meant relying on him. He was the one person she couldn't stand to see her desperate.

He was the only one who knew just how bad things had been at home. Even when she married David, she'd glossed over her childhood with generalizations and platitudes about all she had learned. But Sloan knew the truth, the nitty-gritty of what happened, and to have him be the one to see her back down on her knees was almost too much to bear, especially with him asking questions about her relationship with David.

These past thirteen years, she'd tried not to think of Sloan at all. Usually, she succeeded. She'd been so angry when they broke up, so dejected and hurt, and seeing him again brought her right back to the moment he left. She had loved him with every fiber of her being. He was just having fun.

She sank to the floor and leaned back against the wall, pulling her nightgown over her knees and letting herself remember. Sloan was going to basic training in a week. They'd planned to ask Sloan's mom if Jo could stay here in the house to finish out her last year of high school, but before they got the chance, Evelyn announced she was going on a whirlwind European adventure.

Jo had listened to the details with mounting anxiety, sharing the occasional worried stare with Sloan across the table. "I could house-sit for you," she offered.

"Aw, thank you, sweetie, but it's all taken care of. Louise down at the YMCA has a cousin who needed housing for the summer. I've rented it to him and his family, so I'm all set."

Later that night, Sloan held her cradled against his chest. "So you'll come with me to basic. Get an apartment. I'm sure you can find a waitressing job out there just as easily as you can here."

"I won't be able to afford an apartment on tips."

"And I won't be able to help out until I'm through basic, then advanced training and BUDS. You could stay here and get a place of your own."

"When school starts next week, I won't be able to work enough hours to afford it."

"You could drop out, at least for now."

"Are you kidding?"

He stroked her back. "I don't think there's an easy solution."

She bit her lip. She could think of one that would make all their problems disappear, in addition to making her happy. "We could get married."

His hand stopped moving. "What, like now?"

She propped herself up on her elbow. "Why not? We'd be husband and wife. We wouldn't have to sneak around when we got back. Your mom would let me live here, or she'd help us afford a place until we got on our feet. I'd never have to go back to my dad's. We could make a real home."

"We're a little young to get married."

"Plenty of people get married at our age."

He unhooked his arm from around her shoulders and sat up. "You're serious."

"Of course I am."

"Jo, you know I love you. But I don't want to get married. Not yet, anyway. Are things really that bad at your dad's?"

She felt like she'd been slapped. "You know the answer to that."

"Your uncle's been gone a long time."

"That isn't the point! I don't want to be there."

"And I don't want to go to basic and leave you, but we have to find some way to get through this. Even if it's not ideal, it's an option."

"That isn't fair."

"It isn't fair to assume my mother will pay for us to live if we got married. Jesus, Jo, how can we get married when we can't even support ourselves?"

Her cheeks flushed hot. "We would find a way to make it work."

"On somebody else's dime. No, thank you."

"That's all you can think about? The money?"

"Easy for you to say."

"What does that mean?"

He ran a hand through his hair. "Forget it."

"Because my family's poor. Right? Is that it? My family's poor, so I don't get to tell your family what to do with their money." She got up, picking her clothes up off the floor and hastily getting dressed.

"Okay, yes. We come from very different backgrounds."

She blew out air and wrestled with her sneaker. "Oh, just say it. I'm not good enough for you, and I never was. Trailer trash. You were never going to marry Old Man Buckley's daughter."

"Stop getting dressed. Let's talk about this."

"What is there to talk about? I just got a real good look into your heart, and I don't like what I see."

"You know I love you."

"Do you?" She pulled her sweatshirt over her head. "Do

you love me enough to marry me and take me away from this place?"

He said nothing, only stared at her from across the room. She moved to the door. "Don't call me. Don't come to the diner and see me. In two weeks, you'll be gone and finally free of me."

She wanted him to argue with her, to insist he was wrong and whisper apologies into her hair. Instead, he said, "We could use the time to think about what we really want."

She could still feel the devastation his words wrought inside her. Her world had been shattered that night, leaving her surrounded by shards with no way to fix it. A tear slipped down her cheek. A draft crept around the old window, and she hugged herself against the cold. Some things never changed, and she was grateful this house, at least, was one of them.

7

"Don't finish all the Cap'n Crunch!"

"I got it first."

"That's not fair."

"First come, first serve. It's perfectly fair."

Sloan's eyes popped open, confusion permeating the thick haze of sleep. He stared at his living room ceiling. He was on the couch, and there were children in his kitchen.

Joanne's children.

He sat up slowly, looking around. A pair of sneakers sat in the middle of the floor, one upside down. He scratched the back of his head and sighed, reaching for his prosthetic arm and securing it in place. His head ached a little from the scotch, and he longed for a cup of coffee to take the edge off the pain.

More screaming from the kitchen. "Give that back!"

"You finished the Cap'n Crunch, so I'm taking the Lucky Charms." That was the girl... April. He got up and stretched.

"*Mom!*" yelled the boy.

"Just shut up and eat the Cheerios."

"I hate Cheerios! And don't tell me to shut up!"

Sloan had slept in his jeans, but he pulled on his T-shirt in an attempt to appear presentable as he dove into the fray in the kitchen. "Everyone hates Cheerios. I'd go for the Cap'n Crunch."

The boy didn't miss a beat. *Lucas.* "She touched it. I don't want it after she touched it."

April gestured dramatically. "I poured it from the box into the bowl."

Lucas straightened his arms by his sides, fingers balled into fists. "I'm not eating that crap!"

Sloan held up a hand. "Watch your mouth." He reached into the top of the pantry and dug behind boxes of macaroni and cheese, withdrawing a second box of Lucky Charms. "Here. I'm always prepared."

A single clap behind Sloan made him turn around. Little Fiona stood in the doorway, beaming. "Marshmallows!" God, she was cute. "I don't want milk." She wagged a finger at Sloan and settled at the table.

"If you don't give her milk, she'll only eat the marshmallows," said April.

Sloan nodded. "C'mon, we'll all have them with milk. You want some, right, Lucas?"

"Yeah." The kid pulled out a chair, the sound of chewing soon replacing the chaos.

Sloan poured his own bowl of cereal, momentarily torn. Usually, he just ate the marshmallows. He frowned. "Will you pass the milk, please?" He'd planned on doing some laundry and watching the football game at the bar this afternoon, but that plan was obviously thrown out the window. He picked the marshmallows out of their milky bath, careful to avoid the twiggy parts. "Where's your mom?"

"She's still sleeping," said Lucas, his mouth full of cereal. "What happened to your arm?"

"Lucas!" snapped April.

Sloan held up a hand. "It's okay. I lost it in an accident when I was in the Navy."

The boy grinned. "Did it get sawed off?"

April smacked his arm. "Lucas!"

"No, it—"

Lucas's eyes lit. "Was there an explosion?"

"No—"

"Did you get shot?"

April rolled her eyes and moved to the sink, rinsing out her bowl, while Sloan tried again to answer. "Nothing like that. I was—"

"Ooh, did it get run over by a Humvee?"

Sloan leaned back in his chair. "Nope."

"Did somebody stab you?"

"Nope." He smiled at Fiona, who seemed truly interested in their conversation and not at all disturbed.

"Somebody shot my dad," she said, putting her lips on the edge of the bowl to scoop marshmallows into her mouth.

Sloan turned to the girl, suddenly interested.

"Shut up," yelled Lucas.

Fiona slurped up a diamond-shaped marshmallow, her eyes never leaving Sloan's. "He's in heaven with the angels."

Jesus Christ.

Sloan didn't know what he'd been expecting, but it certainly wasn't this. David had been murdered?

"There's no such thing as heaven," said Lucas, picking up his bowl and dropping it into the sink with a clang.

"Yes, there is! Mommy said so."

"She lied," said Lucas, storming out of the kitchen.

The little girl's face fell and her bottom lip quivered.

"Lucas," snapped Sloan, but the boy was already gone. He squeezed Fiona's arm. "He's just kidding, honey. Of course there's a heaven."

"Do you promise?"

"Absolutely." The girl seemed to accept that and went back to eating, clearly trying to avoid anything that wasn't a marshmallow.

He stood and made coffee, careful to keep his distance from April. She had the air of a frightened animal, and he didn't want her to bolt. On the contrary, he wanted information. "I'm sorry to hear about your dad. How long ago did he pass away?"

"Thursday."

Fuck, no wonder Jo was a wreck. "I'm sorry," he repeated. There was definitely a connection between David's death and Jo's sudden need for money, and he wondered if the other man had left an insurance policy to provide for his family. "What happened?"

The girl shrugged. "We don't know. He was at his hunting cabin."

"So it was an accident?"

April looked pointedly at Fiona, then back at Sloan. "No."

"I see," he said, but he didn't really understand at all. He'd have to have Moto look into it for him. "Where do you live?"

"Just outside of Chicago."

He pulled out his phone and texted Moto, who'd just gone on assignment with Trace out in Wyoming, but hopefully he could find some time to learn what really happened to David Regan.

Joanne appeared in the doorway. "I can't believe I slept

so late." She kissed the top of Fiona's head. "Lucky Charms, eh? Your favorite."

"Marshmallows," said the girl.

Jo headed for the coffeepot. "Morning, April."

"Lucas was being a jerk."

"I heard that!" Lucas yelled from the other room.

"Why don't you hop in the shower?" Jo said, combing the girl's hair back from her face with her fingers. "We're going to get out of here in the next hour or so."

Fiona perked up. "We're going home?"

"No, genius, we can't go home, remember?" asked Lucas as he walked into the room. "And I was not being a jerk. April refused to share the good cereal."

April held up her hands. "I'm going in the shower. I can't take this anymore."

Lucas moved his head back and forth. "Good, 'cause you stink."

"That's enough," said Joanne.

Sloan handed her the first cup of coffee. "There's half-and-half on the top shelf. You sleep okay?"

"Eventually."

"Can I play in the snow?" asked Lucas.

"Sure," said Jo. "But wear your snow pants. We don't have a lot of clean clothes." Lucas left the room and she turned to Sloan. "What time does the bank open?"

She was certainly in a hurry to get out of here, but his curiosity was piqued. David had died days earlier, Joanne was desperate for money, and she couldn't go home. "They're open now. Why don't you come with me for the ride? It'll give us a chance to talk."

"I can't leave Fiona with Lucas. They'll kill each other."

Sloan winced. "I was hoping we could talk privately."

"I haven't had a private conversation since 2007. I'll grab

her iPad and headphones out of the Porsche. I don't think you'd fit in there. We were like sardines in a can."

Fiona's eyes went wide, her mouth forming the letter O. "I watch princesses?"

"Yes, pumpkin," said Joanne with a smile. "You can watch princesses."

8

Six days.

Acid flooded Joanne's stomach as her anxiety reared to life. She only had six more days to find the money and return it to Bannon.

It had been her first thought when she opened her eyes this morning, the words repeating like a mantra while she brushed her teeth and showered.

Six days.

Six days.

You only have six more days.

She grabbed Fiona's booster seat from the Porsche and strapped the girl tightly into the back of Sloan's Bronco while he cleaned off the windshield. She couldn't breathe, her lungs seemingly stilted by the overwhelming panic in her breast. She needed a plan, and she needed it now.

She slid across the smooth leather passenger seat and waited for Sloan as Fiona softly sang "Let it Go," an appropriate soundtrack as Joanne took in the white and gray scene, desperate to distract herself from her anxiety and calm herself down.

The vehicle was quintessential Sloan, and memories of his old pickup truck and the things they'd done on its narrow bench seat came swiftly to her mind. The night she'd lost her virginity, her heart had been bursting with love so profound she thought it could never die. That felt like a lifetime ago, her own naiveté casting her in a light that was unrecognizable to her now.

Sloan climbed in and started the car. Aerosmith blared, startling her, and he turned it down. "Sorry." The corded muscles of his good arm stood out against his honeyed skin as he backed out of the driveway.

She furrowed her brow. "Where did you get a tan in December?"

"Colombia. I was down there for two weeks hunting down a kidnapped CEO from one of the biggest banks in the world."

She cocked her head. "What did you say you do?"

"I didn't." He smiled, stopping at a red light. "I work for HERO Force, the Hands-on Engagement and Reconnaissance Operations team. A lot of former SEALs working in the private sector."

"So you made it. You became a SEAL."

"Yes, ma'am."

"And now you solve kidnappings." The roads were worse than she would have thought, the tires slipping as the light turned green.

"Not so much solving as ending. More often than not, we pay the ransom for the families and get the person home. You'd be surprised how often it happens, but nobody wants it publicized, especially when it's a key player in a corporation. Tends to scare shareholders."

"I bet it would. Do you just do kidnappings?"

"Nah, we also do private security, personal protection,

that kind of thing. Or, as the name says, reconnaissance. Anything, really."

God, she could use someone like that. "Like Navy SEALs for hire."

"Pretty much."

"So, when you help a family pay a ransom, are the police involved?"

"No. Most kidnappers tend to frown on police involvement. The cases I've been on, the family has made a choice. They could have gone to the authorities, but they decided to meet the kidnappers' demands and work outside the system."

The similarities to her own situation were strong, and the first light of hope broke through the clouds. "And what do you think of that? Is that a smart thing to do?"

"Me? I think it makes sense a lot of the time. If you want to see your loved one again, sometimes you've got to play by their rules. The stakes are just too high."

Could Sloan's company help her? Give her a way to find the money Bannon was looking for, deal with this problem, and protect her family in the meantime? Who was she kidding? She couldn't afford to pay them. She was borrowing money for rent, for God's sake.

He glanced at her. "Why do you ask?"

"Just curious."

He'd been driving down a residential street, but now he swerved to the side of the road and put the SUV in park. "Does that curiosity have anything to do with the reason you can't go home?"

She shot a look at Fiona, who seemed not to notice they'd stopped, arms stretched out like she was freezing the forest. "What makes you think I can't go home?"

"Lucas said so."

She rolled her eyes. "He was being dramatic."

"They told me David died. I'm so sorry."

"Thank you."

"Jo, if you did something—anything—you can count on me to help you find your way."

"Did something? Like what?"

Now he peeked at Fiona. "Can she hear us?"

"Definitely not."

He paused for a beat. "Did you kill him?"

"*What?*"

"I wouldn't judge you. Not if he hurt you."

"I told you, he didn't. And I sure as hell didn't kill him, but thanks for your never-ending faith in me."

"I'm just saying, I would help you. You know that old saying, *friends help you move; good friends help you move bodies.*"

"So, you don't even believe me." She huffed. "Can we go, please? I need to get on the road."

He sighed and pulled back onto the road. "I had to ask."

"No, you didn't. But you did it anyway."

"I want to help, damn it. I need information to do that, and you're not giving it to me. You didn't even tell me David had died, for God's sake. What happened?"

"Hunting accident."

He turned onto Main Street, and they drove in silence until he pulled into the bank parking lot. "This would be a lot easier if you'd tell me the truth."

"What makes you think I'm not?"

"I know you, Buckley. You never could lie worth a damn." He got out and slammed his door.

Prick.

The car had finally warmed up and the heat was blasting. She turned it down with an irritated flick and stared out her window. The older she got, the more she hated winter, and her mind turned to possible places to start over—preferably far south of here.

A car pulled into the spot beside her. Georgia sounded nice, though she'd never actually been there, and she realized she was basing her assessment purely on a mental image of peach trees stretched as far as the eye could see. Florida didn't sound appealing. Maybe Louisiana, or Mississippi. Someplace warm where she and the kids could disappear under the cover of Spanish moss and humidity.

A man got out of the car next to her and she averted her eyes, not wanting to engage. But he tapped on her window, drawing her head up. Richard Bannon stood on the other side of the glass, staring at her.

Icy fear coursed through her veins. How had he found her? He'd followed her here, all the way from Chicago, but that wasn't possible. She'd had her eye on the mirror the whole time and would have known if they'd had a tail, wouldn't she?

He gestured for her to roll down the window and, when it was open a crack, asked, "Are you making progress, Mrs. Regan?"

"How did you get here?"

"You didn't think I was just going to trust you to get back to me in a few days, did you? I wouldn't want you deciding to disappear with my money. I need to protect what's mine."

"Did you follow me?"

"I have my ways." He looked at Fiona in the backseat. "Cute kid. I'd hate for anything bad to happen to her. You've got six days left, Mrs. Regan." He moved to walk away, then bent back to the window. "And I wouldn't go leaving the other two alone like that if I was you."

9

───────

Sloan winked at the teller, a sixty-year-old woman who used to serve him lunch in the school cafeteria. "Twenties will be fine, thanks, Mrs. Martin."

"I don't have that much in my drawer. I'll be back in a jiffy."

Ten thousand dollars in twenty-dollar bills was sure to be a little cumbersome to deal with, but he suspected Jo would prefer the smaller bills. She'd only asked for a few thousand, but he wanted to make sure she had enough, and suspected if he pressed her she would clam up. Talking to her today was like walking barefoot over bird spikes. Her defenses had always run high, and her behavior this morning was no exception.

The teller returned and counted out bills. After this was over and Joanne was on her way, maybe he'd take a vacation. Let his toes sink into the sand someplace warm and forget all about Joanne Buckley and whatever the hell she was hiding.

Like you'll be able to do that.

The thought brought him up short. Of course he'd be

able to forget her. He'd been over her for longer than they'd been together, and nothing was going to change that. Besides, clearly she was knee deep in some kind of mess and wouldn't even tell him what was going on. If he had half a brain in his head, he'd let her go just like she wanted. He sucked his cheeks in.

"Here you go," said the teller, returning with a bound stack of bills. "Want me to count it out for you?"

"No, thanks, I trust you." He took the stack in his hand. Ten thousand dollars. A simple stack of bills. This was all she wanted from him. He turned on his heel.

What was the alternative? He couldn't force her to let him in. She was a grown woman who got to call the shots in her own life, and if that put his back up, it said more about him being a nosey bastard than anything about Joanne. Yes. He should definitely let her get back in that Porsche of hers and drive away.

That car was easily worth well over a hundred grand. Anyone with a car like that shouldn't need to borrow a few thousand dollars, much less drive all the way from Chicago to New York to do it. And it was just days after her husband died, for Christ's sake. She should be in mourning, not desperate for cash and anxious as a bird flying over the ocean.

He rounded the service desk, nodding at a neighbor, more convinced with every step there was more to Jo's situation than met the eye. What kind of person would he be if he just let her walk out the door, ignoring his sense that something was terribly wrong? Lucas had said they couldn't go home. What did Sloan need? A personal invitation to intervene?

He could convince her to stay with him for a while, at least a few days. See if he could get her to open up, even if that meant walking on ice that had barely frozen over. He'd cared for her once. The least he could do was be a true friend to her now, or at least try.

He pushed out of the bank and got into his car.

Jo was frantic. "We have to get back. We shouldn't have left April and Lucas alone."

"What's going on?" He drove out of the parking lot. "Did something happen?"

"Please, just hurry."

"Damn it, Joanne! What the hell is going on?" He swerved through traffic and ran a light as it turned red, his tires fighting for traction on the snow-covered road. "Are you in trouble? Is someone trying to hurt you?"

"I thought I could just get away, that we could start over somewhere new and he wouldn't find us."

"Who?"

"David owed someone millions of dollars and if I don't give it back to him within a week..." She looked over her shoulder at Fiona. When she spoke again, it was a whisper. "He's going to kill one of the children. He said if I went to the police, he'd kill them all."

"Jesus, Joanne, why didn't you tell me?"

"I'm telling you now. He was at the bank."

"Who?"

"The man! Richard Bannon. I think he's a mobster. I'm not honestly sure."

Sloan twisted in his seat. "Just now?"

"I don't know how he found us. I didn't think we were followed. I was careful." She let out a single panicked sob. "He said I shouldn't have left the other two home alone."

"Goddamn it." He drove even faster, passing a minivan over a double yellow line. "They must have put some kind of GPS tracker on your car."

"I didn't intend to bring you into this. I thought with some money I could hide and keep us safe."

"We need HERO Force."

"I can't afford—"

"I've got it." He punched in Mac's number on speed dial. When the old man answered, he barked, "Mac, we've got a problem. I need backup at my house, pronto. As many men as you can spare."

10

―――――――

Sometime between the slalom home from the bank and the arrival of the men from HERO Force, Joanne had lost complete control of the situation. "How do we know they won't just follow us again?" she asked.

Mac paced the length of the kitchen with sure, steady steps. "Friend of mine runs the local state police barracks. He's setting us up with a roadblock at the entrance to the thruway."

The front door opened and one of the SEALs walked in. Jo thought his name was Champion, but they all seemed to have nicknames and she was thoroughly confused. "There's nothing on the Porsche. No transponder, no anything," he said.

"Search their belongings," ordered Mac, the kids moving faster than Jo had ever seen them move, bringing their duffel bags for the man to inspect.

Joanne turned to Sloan. "Are you sure your mom won't mind if we take the RV?"

"Thirty-two feet of freedom has never been more neces-sary. She'd do anything for you. You know that."

Her heart squeezed with emotion. Evelyn Nowak had been more like a mother than Joanne's real mom had ever been, and truth be told, she'd missed Sloan's mom terribly over the years. The idea that she would bend over back-wards to help her and her kids nearly broke her fragile composure.

Mac stopped in front of them. "You're sure this is what you want to do? Not too late to change your mind and go to the police."

They'd been discussing this for hours, both before Mac and his team arrived and after. Jo had limited options. Try to find the money and return it to its rightful owner, go to the authorities, or do as she'd originally planned and run away. While that was her favorite option, she could see the wisdom in looking for the money first, and with Sloan and HERO Force on her side, there was actually a chance she'd find it.

Already, their computer guy was working on tracing David's accounts and searching for others, but so far, he hadn't found any money. "I'm afraid to go back there. I keep seeing my house all torn up, knowing someone was in there."

"You'll have me there with you, and the other men near-by," said Sloan. "And you won't need to go home. They can search your house without you being there. You can show us all the places David hung out and we can look for clues."

She nodded. It sounded like a simple enough plan, but inherently dangerous, and she wondered if she'd ever sleep again. "I know. We've been through it all. I'm just worried."

"There's nothing in here," said Champion. "I'd like to take your cell phones apart, any other devices.

Jo handed hers over, as did April. Fiona held up her beloved iPad. The poor kids, they must be at least as frightened as she was, yet they were holding up like champs. While she didn't tell them their lives had been threatened, she did come clean about the man who wanted back the money Daddy had borrowed. "It's going to be okay, guys," she said with more certainty than she felt.

April walked to her and opened her arms, the rare hug making Jo feel there was hope for them yet. The last year with April had been difficult, with the girl becoming more defiant and argumentative. She could only hope their current ordeal would bring them closer together instead of further apart, and the hug was a step in the right direction.

"Nothing in here, either," said Champion. "Could be some kind of tracking software, though."

Sloan nodded. "We need to destroy the phones."

"My 'Pad, too?" asked Fiona, her bottom lip sticking out.

"Yes, sweetie, I'm sorry." He squatted down in front of her. "We need to make sure we stay safe, and there could be something on there that puts us in danger." The little girl nodded, her face a mixture of resolute acceptance and quivering loss, and Sloan knew he had to buy her another iPad at the earliest opportunity.

"It's time," said Mac.

Champion got on his phone. "Chop, they're coming out to load the RV." He'd been watching the house from the road to make sure no one else did the same.

"Won't take long," said Sloan. "All we've got is one bag each and a mangy ol' husky."

Jo nudged him with her elbow. "Don't make fun of my dog."

Sloan met her stare, intensity flashing in their depths

before he grinned. "Who would have thought one day I'd ever choose a Winnebago over a Porsche?"

"I know, right? I call shotgun."

"You're my official copilot. You'd better ride shotgun."

She smiled, suddenly noticing all eyes were on Sloan and her. Mac had stopped pacing and stood with his head cocked, Champion was openly staring, and all three kids looked like they were watching a pig fly across the sky. Her cheeks heated, and she pushed off the counter. "Okay, kids, let's get this show on the road."

11

———————

Sloan drove along the highway, Joanne by his side and the kids tucked into the back of the vehicle, classic rock playing softly on the radio. Fiona had fallen asleep with her new iPad on her lap, April had been playing on her new phone since they left New York, and Lucas was completely engrossed in his Nintendo Switch. The devices were expensive, but he didn't care.

Joanne had quite a fight with April over putting Instagram on her new phone, going so far as to forbid the girl from installing it. Sloan witnessed the legendary wrath of an eleven-year-old girl, and quietly wagered April would install it anyway.

They selected a campground an hour outside of Chicago to stay in overnight. Between the impending reservation and the long, quiet drive, he couldn't help but feel like he was living someone else's life, that these were his kids, this was his wife, and they were traveling on some special vacation.

It was a stupid fantasy and one he wouldn't have admitted to if Joanne had asked what he was thinking. There was just the peaceful feel of sharing each other's company and Sloan's profound sadness at what might have been.

What if he'd said yes all those years ago, instead of freezing up like the idiot he'd been? It hadn't taken him long to realize he'd made the wrong choice in refusing to marry her. Within two weeks of his arrival at basic training, he'd already bought the ring. If he'd gone to her then or called and apologized, told her he was an asshole and a jerk and a hundred different things, he could have begged to have her back. Maybe she wouldn't have married David, and their entire lives would have been different.

But that's not what he did.

He'd choked. He'd dug in his heels. He'd arrogantly thought he'd have the rest of his life to make it up to her. He'd dragged his feet and taken his time and planned exactly how he wanted to pop the question, never imagining she would already be someone else's wife by the time he returned from training.

"Tell me about David." The words were out before he could stop them, the need to know what happened outweighing his desire to maintain the peace. The air between them changed instantly, seeming to carry a charge like a storm blowing in.

"What do you want to know?"

"You got married pretty quick. Why?"

She didn't say anything for the better part of a mile. He knew because he was counting the markers, waiting for her to speak.

"I thought it was the right thing to do."

The right thing to do? "Were you pregnant or something?"

She sighed heavily. "No. You were gone. I was living in

my father's house. Things were worse than they'd ever been. David was nice to me."

"So what, you just married him? Like hey, boom, want to get hitched?"

"Stop it. You have no idea what you're talking about."

Goddamn, he was frustrated, and he would have punched the steering wheel with his hand if it wouldn't have woken Fiona. He wanted answers, and all she wasn't telling him was what he really wanted to know. "Did you love him?"

His hands were sweaty on the wheel, his heart racing. This mattered to him more than it should, but he couldn't back away from the conversation any more than he could stop a freight train with his hands. "Because just a few weeks before that, you were supposedly in love with me, remember?"

"I remember we broke up. I remember you didn't want to be with me."

"I was a kid, Jo. I was scared to get married before the ink dried on my high school diploma. That didn't erase two years together. It didn't make my feelings for you go away. But a hot minute after that, you hitched your apple cart to the next guy in line."

He couldn't stop, couldn't hold back the words that demanded to be said. "Tell me you loved him. Tell me you fell madly, crazy, deeply in love with him like you'd never felt for me, and that's why you married the bastard. Because maybe then I wouldn't hate you so much for doing it."

"Why did you hate me? Why did you even care?"

"Because I was in love with you, damn it!" He lowered his voice on the expletive. "And you married somebody else!"

"I wanted to marry you, remember?"

He ran a hand through his hair. "Jesus Christ. This is ridiculous. No, this is maddening. Do you know that? You are maddening. Forget I asked. Forget I said anything."

According to his GPS, they had an hour to go before arriving at the campground. When they got there, he'd take a long walk. Put some distance between himself and this Griswald family vacation. If he was lucky, Joanne would be asleep when he returned, and he might actually get some quiet time alone.

She cleared her throat. "No."

"No, what?"

"I didn't love him. I was desperate. My dad's stepbrother moved back in with us—"

"Uncle Bobby?" *Fuck.* He was a hardcore drunk who grabbed Jo's ass and talked about her tits like he was discussing the weather. He'd damn near raped her when she was fifteen, and her dad didn't even care, which was when Jo started sleeping over at Sloan's house nearly every night.

Her uncle moving back in was the worst possible thing that could have happened to Jo, and he hated himself for not being there to help her. "Jesus, Jo. I'm so sorry."

"I moved out. I found a roommate and a place that wasn't too bad up over a bar on Main Street, and I was doing okay for a little while. I had to drop out of school because I needed to work, but then the diner burned down and I lost my job, anyway."

If he'd known for one second what she was going through, he would have been there in an instant, and he cursed his own stupidity for leaving her alone. But he needed to hear all of it, the entire story. "Go on."

"David was nice to me. He used to come into the diner, then when that burned down, he showed up at my house.

He brought me flowers. He stood there in his chinos and button-down shirt, talking to my drunk-ass father like it was a totally normal conversation.

"I was so damn sad," she said quietly. "David was there for me. He was going to college in Chicago and wanted me to come with him. He wanted to marry me. I wanted a new life, Sloan. One where I wasn't the poor kid from the wrong side of town, I wasn't just a high school dropout, alone. I saw the chance for a fresh start with a man who loved me, and I took it."

He could hear the tears in her voice, feel the mirrored tension in his own tight throat, and he swallowed against it. "I came back for you."

"What?"

Why was he telling her this now? Nothing good could come of it. The past was the past. It couldn't be changed. But it was clear to him he'd been holding on to it, refusing to let go of the woman who'd given up on him so easily.

There had been no serious relationships in his life, and while he'd told himself it was because he liked to keep things light, not be weighed down, he could see now that was utter bullshit. Once bitten, twice shy. It was time to let this wound heal so he could have a real life for himself, unravel this knot and move on. Maybe have an RV full of his own kids one day.

He looked away from the road to meet her stare, then turned back. He needed to finish this once and for all. "When my training ended. I came home from basic with a ring in my hand. I came back for you, Buckley."

12

With those six words, Sloan took Joanne's entire history and turned it on its head. The past thirteen years had seemed like an inevitable course of events, every decision forcing her into another situation where she had no control over what would happen next.

She stared out her window as they drove into the dark campground, the winding road white with salt residue and flanked by snow-covered evergreens. They came to a small parking lot and Sloan got out to register, her eyes fixing on a fallen tree at the edge of the forest.

Once, she'd stood tall as those trees, believing in herself and the possibilities. But she'd married David in a blind leap of desperation, needing an escape route from her home life and grabbing on to him like a life preserver in a storm. There'd been nothing but emptiness after Sloan left, no hope for any improvement in the future. At least with David, there'd been a chance.

She could see now, she should have been stronger, should have stood tall on her own instead of marrying him to escape. But David's offer had played off Sloan's rejection in her mind like the perfect cure for the hole in her heart. Life had taken away one man but had given her another.

How foolish she'd been.

Her eyes burned, but she held the tears at bay, refusing to bend under the weight of this revelation. Sloan had come back for her. He had loved her, after all.

The words were crushing, making her feel like she couldn't breathe despite the air that filled her lungs and rushed out again. It was such a shame, a waste, an ironic twist of fate, and she wondered what terrible thing she must have done to deserve it.

She ached to hold on to him, to fall apart and let him shore her up like he used to, to have him tell her everything would be okay, to lean into his body and take strength from it. But she couldn't do it. That kind of weakness had knocked her life off course, the desire to be protected forever paramount over the desire to stand straight and tall.

She had to do better this time. Her life and her children's lives were at stake. It was time to be brave, even if that meant being alone.

The driver's door opened, the cold air blowing in as Sloan sat down. "Only two other campers in the whole place. We've got half the lake to ourselves." He drove to a three-sided shed some fifty feet up the road, a lighted wreath gracing its peak and the inside stacked high with firewood, and got out again.

Her mind worked to pull up the date. December eighteenth, seven days until Christmas. She couldn't even wrap her head around the idea that it was Christmastime.

"I don't see why we have to stay here," said April. "Who goes camping in December?"

Joanne forced a lightness into her tone she didn't feel. "We have a Winnebago. It seemed like a good idea."

"Not to me."

Jo squeezed her eyes shut. "Let's just make the best of it, okay?"

"Why are we even with this guy?"

"Who, Sloan?"

"No, the other strange man you hunted down then brought with us back to Chicago."

Joanne turned around. "He's helping us, and I, for one, am very glad he's here."

April bobbed her head. "Yeah, I could tell when you two were talking."

So, that's what the attitude was about. She'd overheard their conversation. The very last thing Jo wanted to do was talk about her love life with her eleven-year-old daughter, but apparently she needed to do it anyway. "Are you upset about something you overheard?"

April rolled her eyes and looked out her window. "Forget it."

Sloan finished loading wood and they drove to their campsite. "I'm just going to level out the camper," he said.

"Can I come?" asked Lucas, bounding up from the back of the RV.

"Sure thing, sport."

Jo considered getting out, too, just to avoid a run-in with April, but didn't act fast enough.

"So what was he, like, your boyfriend? This is the guy you told me about."

Shit. There was no way around this mess. She needed to go straight through. "Yes."

"Is he still?"

"Of course not."

"But you wanted to marry him instead of Dad. Because that's no big deal," she added sarcastically. "I'm sure everybody's mom married their second choice of a husband."

She hesitated, unsure of exactly where this was going and suddenly feeling like she was walking through a minefield. "It's complicated, April."

"Doesn't seem complicated to me. You had very strong feelings for him when you were young. I totally get that, because I'm young and I have strong feelings, too."

"So, that's what this is about. I was not eleven at the time, young lady. Sloan and I didn't start dating until we were fifteen."

"Which is, like, a whole thousand days older than I am, so a totally different situation. Right. I couldn't possibly understand real feelings a thousand days before you did. Oh, wait! Yes, I could, because I'm not a little kid anymore."

Joanne rolled her eyes. "I am so not up for this right now."

"Well, I'm sorry if my timing isn't convenient, Mother."

The patronizing tone in her daughter's voice had Jo spinning around and pointing her finger. "Look, me falling in love at fifteen is not the same thing as you professing your love to a complete stranger on Instagram!"

"He is not a stranger!" She held up her phone.

Jo grabbed the device. "Absolutely ridiculous." She scrolled through the applications.

"Give that back!"

"Did you already install it? Who am I kidding, it was the first thing you did, right?" She shook her head, irritation with herself far greater than her annoyance with her child. She should have realized April would go right back to her conversation at the first opportunity.

There it was, the familiar icon winking back at her, and

with a frustrated jab, she deleted it. "You just lost your phone."

"Mom!"

Sloan pulled open his door. "All set."

She kept yelling at April. "Clearly, you can't be trusted. I'm so freaking angry right now."

"What's the matter?"

Jo hopped out of the camper, desperately needing to get away from her daughter before she exploded. Lucas was arranging logs in the fire pit, Christmas music already playing on a small boom box, and she turned on Sloan. "You realize it's, like, thirty-five degrees out here? Isn't it a little cold for a fire?"

"Almost forty." He smiled. "You watched me load the firewood. What did you think I was going to do with it?"

"I wasn't thinking."

Lucas whined, "Can't we please, Mom? Sloan says we can make s'mores."

Just like camp! The boy was so excited, and some part of her resented that Sloan was mister fun and games, while she was the fun ender, afraid for their lives. "Fine. Sure. Whatever."

Sloan touched her back, and she jerked away.

He furrowed his brow. "What's wrong?"

"Nothing. Just go ahead and make your fire." He crossed to Lucas and instructed him on how to stack the logs so the fire would get plenty of oxygen. David would have made the fire himself or been such a perfectionist about how it should be done that the activity would barely have been fun for Lucas. But Sloan had a way with the boy that clearly said he understood children, and the difference between him and the man she'd married was like salt pressed deep into a festering wound.

She turned away, needing space but unable to go back into the camper without another run-in with April. "I'm going for a walk."

"Wait." Sloan handed Lucas a lighter and showed him where to light the fire, earning the boy a pat on the back and a proud smile. "Great job, kid. Grab the marshmallows out of the back of the camper."

Joanne barely resisted the urge to scream. Sloan jogged to her. "I'll come with you."

"I don't want you to come with me. I want to be alone."

"What happened? Did I miss something?"

She huffed. "April and I were fighting, then you're out here with your father-of-the-year routine, and I'm about to lose my shit."

"What? You're mad at me? What did I do?"

"God, just leave me alone."

"Lucas," he called. "We're going for a walk. Keep an eye on the fire."

"What part of *leave me alone* did you not understand?"

He put his hand on her back and guided her away from their campsite. "If you're pissed at me, I'd like to know why."

"I told you why!"

"Because I'm being nice to your kids?"

"Yes. And the s'mores, and the fire-making lessons."

"That makes no sense at all."

"It makes perfect sense." She swatted his hand off her back. "And stop touching me."

It was her fight with April that had set her off, her insecurities as a parent that had really gotten her going. But how could she make him understand? She pushed the words past the knot that had appeared in her throat. "David would never do that."

"Touch you?"

Heat crept into her cheeks. "No. The way you helped Lucas make a fire. He wouldn't do that." He said nothing, the steady rhythm of their footfalls the only sound. "He wasn't good with the kids. He was easily frustrated, and when he got frustrated, he got mean."

"To you, too?"

"Sometimes. Not like my dad did."

"What happened in the camper just now?"

She blew out air. "Which part? The part where she overheard our conversation or the part where she installed Instagram on her new phone?"

He winced. "I thought that might happen."

"It's my own fault. I wasn't watching her phone as much as I should. By the time I found the conversation, things had gone too far. They're talking about meeting up. They call themselves boyfriend and girlfriend."

A chill went through her and she instinctively moved closer to Sloan, her elbow brushing his as they walked. "Then I came outside, and you were running a Boy Scout meeting for my son, and I felt like a bad parent."

"You're not a bad parent."

"I need you to do something for me." She stopped walking and he faced her.

"Anything."

"Don't be nice to them, Sloan. It isn't fair." What she was asking might not be fair, either, but if she was going to make it through the next part of this journey, she needed to lay some ground rules. "They just lost their father, shitty though he may have been. I need you to back off."

"How is it unfair to be kind to them?"

"It will just make it harder when you leave. Did you see the way Lucas was looking at you back there?"

"We were just making a fire."

"No, you were creating a relationship with a vulnerable kid who's so desperate for paternal affection I could cry."

He lifted his hand and touched her cheek. "Jesus, Jo. Why the hell did you stay with this guy?"

She pulled back as if she'd been slapped. "I didn't. We were separated just over a year."

"Why didn't you tell me that?"

"What difference does it make?" She turned away, walking in the opposite direction.

"Don't walk away from me. Talk to me, Buckley."

She spun around. "What do you want me to say? That I spent my entire adult life with a man I didn't love? That marrying him was the biggest mistake of my life? That he was more like my father than I could ever have imagined? Fine. I said it. Now stop rubbing my nose in it. Stop asking me questions I don't want to answer. Stop asking me for details, and for God's sake, don't ask me why I stayed with him. You weren't even there."

"I should have been."

She was breathing heavily, her bottom lip trembling. They stared at each other in the dim light, a cold breeze blowing softly between them. So much time, so many mistakes. But there was heat in his stare, and desire swirled to life in her belly. It was as if, by admitting the truth to him and to herself, she'd knocked down the barrier she'd been fortifying against him.

Sloan.

She ached with a visceral need for this man and was struck by how different her desire for him had become over time. She was a grown woman now. Experience, heartache, and loneliness had left their marks. She understood passion in a way she hadn't back then. She longed to feel the weight of him between her hips, holding her down. To taste the salt on his gleaming skin, to smell his spicy scent as he took control of her body.

He closed the distance between them, his hand slowly moving to grip the swell of her hip, and her breath hitched as blood rushed to her most sensitive places.

She wanted him to kiss her, but he didn't move, those damn eyes fixed on hers. She knew instinctively what he needed, and she lifted her hand to his chest, the puffy nylon of his jacket separating her from what she really wanted to touch. Slowly, she slid her fingers to his warm neck, lightly trailing her nails up and into the softness of his hair.

His head came down and he kissed her, his mouth at once familiar and new, the taste of him exactly as she'd remembered. She pressed her chest against his as his arms came around her, holding her tightly in place as she opened her mouth to his.

I came back for you, Buckley.

Words couldn't change the past, but they could soothe the wound left in its wake. All these years she'd thought he didn't love her; now she was in his arms. She fitted herself more tightly against him, desire and need demanding more.

A growl came from deep in his chest, a primal sound she recognized from their youth, and her breath came fast and hard. He trailed kisses down the column of her neck and nuzzled her ear, a sensation she hadn't felt since the last time they'd made love so long before.

She wanted all of this man, and she wanted him now. Her conscience nagged at her to think of the children, and she could have wept for the loss of freedom that came with motherhood in that instant.

Kisses would have to do.

She unzipped his coat and slipped her hands inside, the heat of his body on her hands like slipping beneath the covers of a lover's bed. He did the same, their jackets open to each other and the sensitive flesh of her nipples raking over the hardness of his chest through their clothes.

He turned them around, a tree pressing into her back as he continued his assault on her good judgment. One hand slipped beneath her shirt to cup her breast through her bra, and she lifted her leg around him.

"Jesus, Jo," he ground out against her, his hardness pressing into her heat. She reveled in the feel of him, the hem of her coat up high and the bark of the tree digging into her back.

"Mom?"

They jumped apart. Lucas stood some fifteen feet away, his brows crumpled together and an accusing stare shooting from his mother to Sloan and back again.

13

Every bone in Sloan's body told him to talk to the boy, but Joanne had asked him to keep his distance, so he lay in his makeshift bed listening to Lucas toss and turn long after the others were asleep.

She'd spoken privately to Lucas right when they returned, but from the forlorn glances the boy kept throwing in Sloan's direction, the talk had done little to ease his pain. It had to be hard to see his mom kissing Sloan so soon after his father's death, even if they were separated. David was barely cold in the ground, and it occurred to Sloan he might be a bastard for doing what he'd done.

That didn't make him sorry for kissing her, Lucas's feelings and sheer bastard-hood aside. Hell, he'd wanted to do a lot more than kiss her, his body remembering every nuance of hers and longing to see if making love to her was as good as he remembered. If her kids hadn't been nearby, he would have taken her right against that tree and found out but good.

He punched his pillow and rolled over, the image of Joanne spread open to him in the woods doing nothing for his insomnia. The dog stood and resettled with his head on Sloan's knee.

Sloan had been intending to help Jo and send her on her way, but now he knew it wouldn't be so simple. They clearly had unfinished business, at least in bed. He thought of the eager way she pressed herself against him from hip to mouth and shuddered. The chemistry between them had always been off the charts, but now it was on fire.

His phone vibrated from the floor beside his bed, and he picked it up, a text message from Moto visible on the home screen and the light from the device illuminating the space.

FOUND TWO ACCOUNTS AT A BANK IN CHICAGO. BOTH CLEANED OUT ON FRIDAY.

He frowned, typing back, REGAN WAS ALREADY DEAD. GET BANK VIDEO.

"Why were you kissing my mom?"

Lucas was sitting upright in his bed just a few feet away.

So much for not talking.

He put down his phone. "Because I like her." He debated how much he should share, briefly considering ending the conversation there and going back to bed. But no matter what Joanne had asked him to do, he couldn't just ignore a kid's questions—especially one who was clearly in pain. "It upset you to see that, huh?"

"Does that mean you love her?"

"People kiss for different reasons."

"She didn't kiss my dad."

Hmm. He'd be lying if he said he didn't want to hear more about that. "Not at all?"

"No. If you don't love her, you shouldn't kiss her, because she might get confused."

One side of Sloan's mouth slid into a smile. "Confused?"

"Yeah. Girls think kissing means you love them. It happened to me with Laney Bastian in second grade."

"What grade are you in now?"

"Third."

"That was a long time ago then."

"Yeah, but still. You've got to be careful."

"I'll remember that."

Lucas was quiet for a minute. "I saw my dad kiss his secretary once, but don't tell my mom because she might get sad."

"You didn't tell her?"

"Dad said kissing is complicated."

"Did they still live together then, your mom and dad?"

"Yeah."

Even in the darkened camper, Sloan could see the strain on the little boy's face. "I'll bet that was hard for you."

Lucas nodded. Sloan looked to the tiny kitchenette. For every crisis, there was a food that could help. "You hungry? I could go for a snack." Lucas hopped out of bed, beating Sloan to the cupboard. After finding a bag of chocolate chip cookies, he poured two glasses of milk, careful not to turn on any lights that might disturb April, and they returned to their beds with their food, eating quietly.

After a minute, Lucas spoke around a mouthful of cookies. "She's not bad."

"Who?"

"My mom. She's nice, and she makes good brownies."

Sloan had no idea where this was going. "Good brownies are important."

"So if you want to love her, you can. Then you can kiss, and she can make you brownies whenever you want."

Sloan nearly choked. He finished chewing and forced

down his food. "Is that what love is about? Kissing and making brownies?"

"You'd have to take out the trash, because that's what the guy does."

"I like to cook. Can I be the cook?"

"Sure. She burns stuff sometimes, so I don't think she'll mind." Lucas drained his milk and looked around for a place to put the glass.

"Here." Sloan held out his hand and returned the glass to the kitchen. "Get some sleep, knucklehead." He turned to go back to his own bed, when a flash of light outside the window caught his eye. Instinctively, he dropped into a squat, leaving just enough of himself exposed to peer out the tiny window, but it was too dark to see anything. He thought of the night vision goggles and weapons he'd packed in the storage area of the camper, which could be accessed from the master bedroom. "Lucas, stay in your bed. Don't get up, okay? I'll be back in a minute."

14

Joanne awoke to a rustling noise behind her head and sat up, trying to get her bearings.

The camper.

The missing money.

David's death.

The kiss she'd shared with Sloan.

Oh, God.

More rustling, and she turned, looking at the sleeping Fiona curled up beside her before leaning over the side of the bed to see where the noise was coming from.

Sloan sat up at the same time. "Sorry I woke you. I need to find my night vision goggles."

He went back into the storage cabinet hidden behind her bed, her eyes focusing on the dark shape outlined by the light vinyl flooring. She gasped. "Is that a gun?"

"Yeah. I saw something outside. I want to check it out."

Fear shot adrenaline into her bloodstream. "Is somebody out there?"

"I don't know yet." He huffed. "I packed my gear so I'd

have easy access. How much stuff did you put in here after that?"

"Just what we needed. There isn't that much."

"This is more than I pack for a month."

"A bachelor and a family of four require a very different amount of stuff. Besides, you'd probably wear one pair of cargo shorts the entire time."

His voice was muffled. "That's called efficiency." The sound of something falling down rumbled from inside the cabinet, then he backed out butt first. "Got it." He stood. "You stay here. Lucas is awake. I'm going to send him back to you on my way out."

"You're going out there?"

"I'll check out the windows first, but yes. It's probably just an animal."

"Really?"

"Not unless that animal has a cell phone. I saw a light."

She balled her hands into fists. "Then why are you telling me it's an animal?"

"Because I don't want you to worry."

"Then why did you tell me you saw a light?"

"Because I didn't want to lie." He winked before pulling the goggles over his head, the action just barely visible in the dark room. "Probably just a neighbor out for a walk. I'll lock the camper door behind me. You stay here."

Her heart was hammering hard. Had they been followed here from Sloan's house despite all their precautions? It didn't seem possible, yet somehow Bannon had found them at the bank in Hyde Park, and that had seemed impossible too. Someone was out there. Maybe it was a park ranger or one of the other campers. Yes, surely, that must be it.

Please, God, let that be it.

Lucas walked into the room and scampered onto her bed. "Sloan has a gun!"

"I know. It's okay. He's in the military." Or at least he used to be. Not that it mattered, if they were all going to die.

We're not going to die!

She had to stop this. Lucas needed her to be calm. She leaned back on the pillows and opened her arm for her son to cuddle with her. "Watch out for your sister."

"Sloan really likes brownies."

She was straining to hear outside. "That's good."

"But he really likes to cook."

"Okay, then, he should make himself some brownies. Now be quiet."

"I told him you make good brownies."

"That's Betty Crocker, but thank you."

"Who?"

"Never mind. I want to be able to hear."

"I don't think he'd mind taking out the trash. He didn't really say."

"What are we talking about?"

"Sloan."

"And his never-ending love for brownies and trash?"

He shrugged. "I like him."

She frowned, grateful he couldn't see her face. She'd seen this coming a mile away, Lucas's quick attachment to Sloan as predictable as the weather. She pulled him closer, wishing she'd given him a better father in the first place, a man he could emulate and love and have that love returned. A man to play baseball with and bake brownies. David had tried, but none of it came naturally to him and he would just get upset.

Stop it.

Being this close to Sloan was getting to her. No, kissing

Sloan had made her lose her mind. A week ago, that man was a painful memory; now here she was, wondering if maybe—just maybe—they could have a future together.

And that was insane. One kiss did not a future make. It was for old times' sake, a necessary evil to satisfy their curiosity so they could move on in different directions. Except it didn't feel evil at all. It felt heavenly.

God, when was the last time she'd been so aroused? The simple touch of his hands on her body and she was desperate for more. What would it be like to actually date him again, to have him in her life and in her bed whenever she wanted him there? To make love and to flirt, to talk deep into the night like they had when they were teenagers?

The kids liked him, at least Fiona and Lucas. She'd been trying to prevent that, yet here they were. Maybe she should embrace it. Let him truly be a part of all their lives and just see what happened. She frowned. He'd already broken her heart once. Did she really want him to break her kids' hearts, too?

The crunch of snow beneath heavy feet could be heard outside the camper, and her stare locked on the window beside the bed.

Probably just a neighbor out for a walk.

Or a giant bear.

Or someone here to kill me.

She felt like a rabbit stopped dead in the road, the grill of a tractor trailer looming. The anxiety that had been her near constant companion locked her joints in place, sure as the rust on the Tin Man.

Maybe it was Sloan, with his night vision goggles and gun, or maybe Richard Bannon had actually tracked them down. Her stomach lurched at the thought, and she squeezed her eyes shut.

No. They'd been careful. HERO Force had made sure they hadn't been followed leaving Sloan's house. It had to be something else. There must be a rational explanation.

Shouting erupted outside the camper and she jumped, the voices deep and male. She and Lucas bolted upright in bed. "What's going on?" he whispered, and she shushed him. There was angry yelling, then a voice that was definitely Sloan's. Should she go out there and help? He'd told her to stay put, but what if he needed her?

Suddenly, the camper rocked, the weight of something slamming into it. Gus started barking and Lucas leaned into her body. "I'm scared."

"I know, sweetie. It's okay. Sloan will take care of it."

"Who's out there?"

"I don't know."

"Did April come back in?"

A high-pitched hum vibrated in her ears, time instantly slowing to a crawl. She lifted his chin, demanding his attention. "What do you mean? April didn't go outside."

"Yes, she did. While Sloan and me were getting cookies."

Jesus Christ!

April was out there, and Sloan had a gun. Gone was her earlier inertia. She flew off the bed. "How long ago was that?"

"I don't know. Like twenty minutes?"

She raced for the door. "Stay with Fiona! Don't come outside!" She fumbled with the lock on the camper door, unable to open it in her desperation to do so. "Sloan!" she screamed as loudly as she could. "April's out there!"

15

—————

Sloan was ambushed from behind, the NVGs ripped from his head and his weapon knocked from his hand. He landed a punch on his attacker, propelling him into the camper, and grabbed his tactical knife from his ankle holster. His attacker advanced, and Sloan got a slice of his arm before being kicked in the groin and going down.

Son of a bitch.

The other man took off. Sloan moved to get up, his good arm grazing the cold metal of his handgun, and he grabbed it before coming to a stand. His hands were steady on his Glock, and two figures centered in his line of vision across the campsite, but without the NVGs, he couldn't see shit. "Put your hands in the air!" The smaller of the two men did as he was told, but the bigger one took off running into the woods. With his weapon trained on the stationary figure, Sloan's finger hesitated over the trigger.

The figure sobbed once, the voice high, like a woman's. "It's me, April."

A huge wave of protectiveness crashed over him. He hadn't even known she was outside, and she'd been in danger—first from her attacker and then from himself. "Stay there!" He flew back into search mode, scanning the area for the tango who'd gotten away, spotting a figure running across a clearing some hundred yards away, outlined by the white snow. He aimed his weapon.

"No!" screamed April. "He's my friend!"

His limbs continued to move as his brain took a moment to comprehend, Joanne's story about April's online boyfriend forcing the pieces into place. He stopped running and turned around. "Are you fucking kidding me?"

"No. It's okay."

"Instagram?"

"Yeah," she said meekly, tears evident in her voice.

"For a nice guy, he packs a hell of a punch. Why the fuck did he come after me, then?"

"You scared us with your gun and that thing on your head!"

"Damn it, April, you scared me." He walked slowly back to her, his hands on his hips. "What the hell was he doing here?"

She shrugged, still crying. "I wanted to see him. He lives nearby."

"Then you tell somebody. You don't just sneak out of the camper at night and let me think we're being attacked, for God's sake." He was yelling and she was already upset, but he couldn't seem to stop himself. What if things had gone down differently and he'd used his Glock, never knowing it was her? Or what if his goddamn prosthetic had gotten her killed? The possibility had his hand shaking. "Do you realize what could have happened?"

"I just wanted to meet him, and I knew Mom wouldn't let me. I didn't think you'd come after us with a gun!"

Her fear was evident in her voice, and he finally took a

moment to see things from her point of view. She wasn't even a teenager, she was just a kid. She wanted to see this boy and resorted to sneaking out as millions of girls had done before her.

He'd come after them with headgear and a Glock.

No wonder the poor thing was terrified.

He opened his arms. "Come here." She didn't budge, and his arms fell to his sides. "I'm sorry. I knew someone was out here and I needed to protect your mother."

"You scared the crap out of me."

"I know. I'm sorry. I think I cut your friend's arm."

"Bad?"

"I don't think so. I don't know." She wiped her eyes and nose with one swipe, the gesture so childlike he was struck by the awkwardness of her age. "Come on. Let's go in to your mother. She's got to be worried sick by now."

She sighed. "Mom's awake?"

"Most definitely."

She fell into step beside him. "You're not going to tell her."

"Of course I am."

"She's going to kill me."

"Probably."

"She's never going to give me my phone back."

"Absolutely not." He picked up his NVGs and brushed off snow and dirt. "There are cookies on the counter. Milk's in the fridge."

The door of the camper rattled dramatically. "April's out there!" Jo yelled.

"Calm down, I know. I've got her. Let go of the handle."

"Don't shoot her!"

"Jo, calm down. Let go of the door." He reached in his pocket and withdrew the key, then unlocked the door and opened it. She all but fell out of the RV and pulled April into her arms. "Are you all right?"

"I'm fine."

"What were you doing out here late at night? You scared the hell out of us!"

April pulled back. "I was meeting my friend."

"*What?*"

Sloan put his arm on Jo's back. "It's cold out here. Let's talk inside." He could feel the tension in her body, about to unleash. Joanne was going to lay into April but good. "Godspeed," he whispered under his breath, following the pair inside.

All hell broke loose at that point, and Sloan quietly picked up his phone and retreated to the bedroom, perching on the edge of the bed beside the sleeping Fiona and checking his messages. Moto had answered him.

ALREADY GOT IT. THIS THE WIFE?

A video file was attached. "Fuck," he whispered, hitting play.

"What's the matter?" asked Lucas, crossing to his side.

"I shouldn't have said that. Didn't see you there." A woman entered the picture, but it was too far away to see her face clearly.

"Mom's screaming at April. I'm staying away. What are you watching?"

"A surveillance video. Just take a sec."

Lucas leaned over the screen. "That a bank?"

"Yeah."

"Who is she?"

"I don't know."

The camera angle switched to a shot from the teller's point of view, the woman's face now clearly visible. It wasn't Jo, and Sloan released a breath he hadn't realized he'd been holding. He'd been afraid she had been lying to him, and it was a relief to realize she was not. He flicked off the video.

Lucas's expression was dark, his stare boring into Sloan's.

"What's wrong, kiddo?" Sloan asked.

"That's her."

He furrowed his brow. "Who?"

"The woman my dad was kissing."

16

Joanne dug a roll of antacids from her purse. "I don't like getting this close to Richard Bannon on purpose."

"It's his wife's office, not his."

"That's still too close." She bit down on the chalky tablet. She was cranky, having gotten little sleep last night after April's escapades and Sloan sharing the video of McKenzie at the bank. Jo's mind had been full of questions and possible scenarios that could explain why David's former lover would be withdrawing large sums of money after he died.

If he'd died at all.

Bannon had claimed to have killed him, but what if that was a lie to make her believe he was capable of hurting her kids? The thought had begun to percolate the moment she'd seen the video, regardless of the body in the casket they had buried. Someone had died in that hunting cabin, and she'd assumed it had been David. But what if she'd been wrong? What if they were all wrong?

David was having an affair with Bannon's wife, and if he

wasn't really dead, that gave them both an entirely different motivation. Maybe he was alive and well and living on the beach with McKenzie somewhere.

According to Moto at HERO Force, David had several joint bank accounts with his former secretary, which was why she was able to withdraw the money. McKenzie was the key, the answer to this riddle that had turned Jo's world upside down, and she wasn't sure if she was hoping to find the other woman at work or not. "What if he's alive?"

Sloan sighed heavily. "I was wondering the same thing. Between the money and the mistress, it's looking like he had plenty of reason to fake his own death."

"But there's a body. If David's alive, who died in that fire?"

"Impossible to say."

"This is unbelievable. And we're running out of time."

"Don't panic. We're working on it. HERO Force is doing all they can to find out more about McKenzie's financial records." They drove to the opposite side of the city and exited the expressway in an expensive suburb. "How well did you know her?"

Jo shrugged. "Not well. She came over to the house a few times to work on projects with David on weekends. He had a home office." How foolish she'd been then. She glanced over her shoulder to be sure the kids couldn't hear their conversation, finding them engrossed in their electronics. "They probably had fuck parties in there while I was knocking politely and bringing them coffee."

"Fuck parties?"

"Yes."

"I don't think I've ever been to a fuck party."

"You know what I mean."

He turned down a quaint little main street lined with

glass-fronted businesses. "That's it, next to the coffee shop. Number fourteen-twelve." He pulled into a parking spot.

Joanne unbuckled her seat belt. "What are we going to say to this woman? Excuse me, but I know you were boffing my husband. Were you also stealing money from yours and planning a dramatic getaway? Oh, and by the way, any chance David's still alive and hiding out in your basement?"

"Something like that."

"Can I come in?" piped Lucas.

"No," Sloan and Joanne said in unison.

"Can I get gum?" he asked.

"They don't sell gum at interior decorating firms. We'll only be a few minutes," she added, opening her door and climbing down from the high seat onto a sidewalk dusted with fresh snow. Next door, an older woman watched them with open curiosity from the wide window of a knitting shop.

Sloan met Jo beside the camper. "Neighborhood watch," he said, indicating the woman and offering her a friendly wave.

"Best security system around." She followed him to the door. "I hate this."

"You can wait in the camper."

"No way." He pulled the door handle, finding it locked, and rang the doorbell. Joanne's heart was beating like a ticking clock. When no one answered, he cupped his hands around his eyes and peered inside. "Looks like they're closed." Desks were clear, and shelves that looked like they should be stocked stood bare. "Looks like they've been closed for a while. Ten bucks says the knitting lady knows what's up."

"Should we ask her?"

"Yeah. Pretend you're tight with McKenzie. You can say you used to work with her at David's accounting firm."

"Oh, God, don't make me lie." She turned and headed next door.

"Really doesn't come naturally to you, does it?"

"You know it doesn't."

"Just a little white lie. No big deal. You smile and say, 'Do you know when McKenzie will be back in the office? I used to work with her at...' What's the name of the firm?"

"Baldwin & Regan."

He rolled his eyes. "Of course it is. So, 'I used to work with her at Baldwin & Regan. My husband and I just happened to be passing through town—'"

"Husband?"

He shrugged. "Why not? Easiest way to explain me being here."

"I'd rather say literally anything else."

"Who else would you be traveling with?"

"I don't know, but there's no way you're going to be my husband in this scenario." He could be her pimp or even her parole officer. Anything but her husband.

"We got married in the Florida Keys," he said. "Very spur-of-the-moment. Honeymooned in the South of France. The kids were thrilled, of course."

She gave him her best stink eye, then pulled open the door of the knitting shop. The woman from the window pulled her cardigan closed against the cold. "May I help you?"

Lying made Jo physically sick, her stomach heaving as she forced a smile onto her face and pushed ahead. "We're looking for McKenzie Bannon. I used to work with her. Do you have any idea when she might be back?"

"No, I'm afraid I don't."

Sloan laughed good-naturedly. "Oh, honey, you sound like a burglar, for goodness' sake. My wife sometimes forgets the world is a dangerous place. Am I right?" The woman looked less than convinced.

"We're friends from Baldwin & Regan," he continued. "Well, Suzie here is. I only met McKenzie a few times when we went out for dinner in the city. Super nice girl." He put his hand on Joanne's back. She bristled at his touch but resisted the urge to shake him off. "I've got three kids from my first marriage who were still reeling from losing their momma. Suzie here quit her job to be there for them, and we took off cross country!"

The old woman's eyes lit. "Doesn't that sound exciting. Have you been at it long?"

"It'll be a year and a half a week from next Monday. Best thing we ever did, wasn't it, sweetheart?" He looked lovingly at Jo, and she grinned while wishing she could punch him in the mouth.

"Oh, absolutely. Yellowstone was my favorite."

"Yellowstone is everyone's favorite," said the woman with a smile. "I always dreamed of going myself."

"It's never too late," said Sloan, his voice dripping with saccharin sweetness. "Especially with the right person by your side." He lifted Jo's hand to his mouth and kissed it, the gesture sparking a thrill in Jo's belly that she instantly hated him for igniting.

"Anyway," he continued. "If you know how we might catch up with McKenzie, we'd sure appreciate it."

"Unfortunately, I don't know that she'll be back, at least not for quite some time. Her father passed away, and she was heading to Poughkeepsie to close up his plumbing supply business. She said she needed to take some time. Death in the family will do that to a person."

Jo and Sloan shared a look, then thanked her and said their goodbyes. Jo led the way back to the camper, her arms crossed and her steps heavier on the pavement than they needed to be. "You just had to be my husband."

She climbed into the cab and pulled so hard on her seat belt it locked up. She cursed under her breath.

"You can't pull it so hard."

"I know!"

"It didn't look like you knew."

"Shut up!" She buckled her seat belt.

"I take it we're going to Poughkeepsie."

She blew out air, turning to check on the children. Fiona had fallen asleep, and Lucas and April both wore headphones. "If he's alive, this is bigger than stealing money from the mob, bigger than threatening me." She lowered her voice. "There was a body in that casket. We could be talking about murder of someone other than David here. But what do we do? We can't call the authorities. I feel like this is getting out of control. Dangerous, even."

"Agreed. And we're traipsing around with three kids in tow."

"What do you suggest?"

He tapped his finger on the steering wheel. "Someplace safe for them to stay. One of the HERO Force guys has a cabin in the northern part of the Hudson Valley, not far from Poughkeepsie. It's closer than my house. They could stay there."

"But who would watch them?"

He turned to her and smiled, then picked up his cell phone. "I know the perfect babysitter." He hit speed dial. "She'll have to cut her trip short, but I'm willing to bet she won't mind."

17

They were going in circles in more ways than one.

Sloan drove the now-familiar highway back from Chicago toward New York, Joanne asleep by his side. He could only hope what he'd said to her was true, and they were really making progress.

Moto had checked into the plumbing supply business, and sure enough, its owner had just recently passed away. It was located in a warehouse on the banks of the Hudson River. It would take twelve hours to drive there.

Fiona and Lucas were struggling with so much time in the camper and needed a break, so they planned to spend the night at a hotel, then pick up Sloan's mother at the Albany airport in the morning before dropping Evelyn and the kids at Wiseman's cabin in the foothills of the Catskills. There they would be safe, while he and Joanne looked for McKenzie and the missing money.

He put in his AirPods and dialed Mac, filling him in on the timetable. "Do you want any men at the cabin?" Mac asked, since HERO Force New York was just over an hour's drive from Wiseman's place.

"Not necessary. No one will know they're there. Just meet us at the warehouse in Poughkeepsie. Who's coming?"

"Champion, Chop, me. Gavin and Asher are flying in from Honduras tomorrow if we need backup."

"Have them come up when they get in. I've got a bad feeling about this one."

"What are you worried about?"

"That it might be a trap." He hadn't voiced that concern to Joanne, but with McKenzie being married to Bannon, anything was possible. "I don't know if we're going to walk in there and find Regan alive or the mob equivalent of a firing squad."

"Got it. I'll have all hands on deck for this one. See if I can bring in Razorback, too."

"Ask Moto to get the plans for the warehouse. I don't like going in there blind."

"Already tried. The building's too old. Nothing on file."

Sloan cursed under his breath. "Tell him thanks for trying."

"Have a safe trip, brother."

Sloan hung up and sighed. So, they'd be going in blind, after all. He wished he could leave Joanne at Wiseman's cabin, too, just to keep her out of harm's way. But as the only one with a relationship with McKenzie, her presence was necessary, no matter how uncomfortable that made him.

Yeah, he had a bad feeling, all right.

He thought of his arm and the recent issues he'd had in combat. If the shit hit the fan at the warehouse, he needed to be at his best, not this eighty-five percent, one-armed soldier bullshit. But that was out of his control, and he knew it. More than that, it scared him. He'd nearly gotten Razorback killed. This time, there was even more on the line.

"I'm hungry," piped Fiona from the back of the camper.

"Me, too," called Lucas.

"Me, too. There's a rest stop a few miles up the way." He eyed April in the rearview mirror, seeming to watch a movie with Fiona on the iPad. The older girl had been downright withdrawn since the incident at the campground, and he didn't know how to pull her out of her funk.

That's because they aren't your kids, asshole.

This was Joanne's family, Joanne's life. Beyond knowing they all liked Lucky Charms, he was just an interloper with no inside information on this clan. But if he was being honest with himself, sometime over the last few days, that was beginning to bother him.

He wanted to be there for Joanne and her kids, wanted to get to know them better. Hell, he even wanted to be closer to April, though that girl's attitude could burn like the sun. He could see himself here, with them, going forward. Could imagine that all of them might one day become a family.

The *Brady Bunch* theme song started playing in his head. *I'm an idiot.*

She'd asked him not to be nice to her kids, now here he was, thinking they might make a nice family. Just add water and stir. But nothing in life was ever as simple as it looked, least of all a woman and kids.

Maybe he could start small. Ask her out on a date. Given that he'd nearly made love to her against a tree, that seemed like the gentlemanly thing to do. Dinner and a movie. No, Joanne hated going to movies with him because they couldn't talk. Dinner and bowling. Dinner and sex. Damn it, the tree idea had taken hold.

"I gotta go potty," called Fiona.

"We're almost there. Five minutes. Can you hold it?"

"No."

"Well, you have to."

"Okay."

He smiled. Road trips were widely considered to be one of the levels of hell, but rather than aggravating him, it only showed Sloan how much he enjoyed their company. Maybe what he'd said to the old woman in the knitting store had held a kernel of truth. Maybe it wasn't too late to grab the brass ring and hang on for the ride. Hell, he's said something similar to Mac just the other day.

There was more between Jo and him than just some left-over chemistry. There was enough of a real relationship left over to build upon. But did she feel the same way? They were almost to the rest stop, and he gently shook her shoulder to wake her up. "We're going to stop up here and get some food."

She sat up slowly and stretched, nodding. "How much farther are we going tonight?"

"Maybe another hour. Fiona's about had it."

"Me, too."

He wanted to talk to her, wanted to see what would happen if he said what was in his head. His palms started sweating. "I was doing some thinking about you and me."

"Oh?"

Just say it. Just push through the bullshit and say it.

"I enjoy your company." *God, that's lame.* "I mean, I like being around you. When we were going back and forth, bickering, I realized how much I missed it."

"Arguing with me?"

"Yeah. Or like, not arguing. Disagreeing."

"We were arguing."

"It doesn't matter. I liked it. That's what matters."

"Okay. So what?"

This is not going well. "So, I guess I was wondering if you liked it, too." *Cringe.* The *thud-thud-thud* of the pavement joints counted out the time it took her to answer. God, he was bad at this.

She sighed. "I don't know."

"You don't know if you liked it?"

She clucked her tongue and looked away. "It's not that simple."

"Of course it is. Did you like it or not? Pretty straightforward to me."

"Don't railroad me, Sloan."

"Asking if you've enjoyed my company like I've enjoyed yours over the last couple of days is not railroading you. It's laying my feelings on the line. Putting myself out there."

"Could you lower your voice, please?"

He did. "What, you don't want your kids to hear that I like spending time with you? I think when this is all over, we should go to dinner."

"Stop. Please."

That was what he got for going out on a limb. One hell of a fall to the ground. She wouldn't even look at him. "Forget I said anything." He changed lanes, the camper slowing down as he approached the rest area.

Sloan's mood hung in the air like a heavy storm cloud. He had his answer. And while his gut told him Jo still had feelings for him, he had no intention of forcing the issue.

18

"Evelyn." Joanne opened her arms and hugged Sloan's mother. They were pulled up to the arrivals curb at the Albany, New York airport, Gus barking his head off inside the camper. "Thanks so much for coming."

The older woman looked stylish in printed capris and a white tank, her once-blonde hair now silvery-white. She smelled like baby powder and perfume, the same scent she always had, and Jo felt happier in that instant than she had in a very long time. Evelyn laughed, leaning back to hold Jo's arms wide. "Look at you! You're all grown up."

"You look great." Jo was smiling so much her face ached. "These are my children." She introduced Lucas and April, who waved uncertainly at the gregarious woman, but Fiona came in close and gave Evelyn a hug.

Sloan hugged her next. "Hi, Ma. Did you have a good trip?"

"Always."

"Sorry you had to cut it short," said Jo. "We really appreciate the help."

"Happy to do it."

Jo offered Evelyn the passenger seat, but she insisted she wanted to get to know the children. Gus attacked Evelyn as Sloan pulled away from the curb. "She's a little desperate for grandchildren."

"Mine could use a grandmother. Maybe we can work out a deal."

"David's mom isn't around?"

"Oh, she's around. Let's just say she isn't grandma material." She twisted around in her seat. "I smell butterscotch."

"She probably loaded her pockets with candy, like a mailman with a pocket full of bacon."

She sighed. "I love your mom."

"She loves you, too."

Joanne stared out her window, watching field after field fly by. She felt better after finally getting a good night's sleep at the hotel last night, whether because of her physical distance from Sloan or Evelyn's impending arrival, she wasn't certain. But she was keenly aware of having lost another day without finding Bannon's money and the growing tension between herself and Sloan.

The latter was her fault. "I'm sorry about yesterday."

"Don't worry about it."

"I do enjoy your company." She sighed, wishing she could give him a very different answer. "I just worry that it isn't going to work out long term. And that's fine for us, but the kids... I don't know how to date with kids, to keep things light and casual so they don't get attached."

"We just tell them we're going to dinner."

She blew out air. "You don't understand. You're like that pocket full of butterscotch, and you don't even know it. You've got each one of them wrapped around your finger just by being you. I need to protect them from getting hurt, and I don't know how to keep them from caring about you."

"They can handle more than you think."

"They just lost their father, Sloan. He and I were separated, but he and the kids were not. Bringing you into their lives right now would be like replacing something they haven't even gotten used to living without."

"You make it sound like I'd step right into his place. That isn't what would happen. No one can replace their father, just like nothing could replace my arm. Do you think I feel for one minute like I'm the same man with a prosthetic that I was with flesh and bone? Letting me into their lives might be a good thing for us all."

She had so much sympathy for all he'd lost in service to his country, but that didn't make his analogy fair or his reasoning sound. "I respectfully disagree. Their needs have to come first for a while."

Laughter came from the back of the camper, where Evelyn was playing a game with the kids. Fiona squealed with delight. "They love her already," he said. "Does that mean you want her to go, too?"

She shook her head. "Of course not. Can you please just respect what I'm saying here, and not pretend the kids playing Uno with your mother is the same thing as you and me dating? I have too much on my plate already, with David and this money and with Bannon. I just can't handle any more."

"You make it sound like I'm part of the problem."

"No. You're going out of your way to help us, and I couldn't be more grateful."

"Grateful."

"Yes."

He drove along for several miles. Had her words stung

him? She found that hard to believe. But he was clearly upset. When he spoke again, he surprised her.

"I'm sorry." He picked up a Twizzler from the open package on the center console. "You're right." He grabbed another and handed it to her. "Truce?"

She took it and nodded, torn between feeling relieved and suspicious. "Truce."

He exited the highway and continued on a winding mountain road, the sun coming out to shine on the winter woods. Her heart was heavy, wishing she could have given him a different answer, but she knew she was making the only choice she could in this circumstance. This wasn't about what she wanted, but what was best for her children.

Sloan picked up his phone and handed it to her. "Can you call one of those car rental places? The one that will pick you up. We could use a car with some get-up-and-go. We'll leave this beast with my mother."

"You sure there's one out here?"

"We're not far from civilization, believe it or not. The address of the cabin is in my wallet."

She picked it up from the console and opened the billfold, doing her best to ignore the outline of what was clearly a condom. She did an internet search on his phone and found he was right, there was a rental car company less than ten miles from here. She placed the call, wondering against her better judgment when he would end up using that condom, and with whom. "They can be at the cabin in an hour."

He nodded, turning off the main road and onto a more narrow one that followed a stream, its water rushing past snow-covered ground and snow-laden trees. The camper rounded a wide turn, a log cabin with a wraparound porch coming into view.

Jo unbuckled her seat belt. "This is beautiful."

"It is." She turned to him, his stare heavy and pointed. He wasn't talking about the cabin, he was talking about her. Her face grew hot. How was she going to stay clear of him once the children were no longer traveling with them? One single look, and she was melting into the ground.

He moved to get out, breaking their connection. "Come on, Buckley, I'll show you around."

19

Joanne pulled a set of plaid flannel sheets out of the linen closet. Sloan said Wiseman's cabin was now an Airbnb and well-stocked and ready for guests. "Fiona should be okay sleeping here with April. But if she wakes up during the night, I usually just let her climb in bed with me. Don't judge." She tossed the fitted sheet over the bed, and Evelyn grabbed the opposite corner, pulling it around the mattress.

"I wouldn't dream of it, dear." Evelyn winked.

"She's been having nightmares lately."

"I imagine so. You've all been through a great deal. I'm sorry for your loss."

"Thank you. We were separated, but it's still hard." The anxiety Jo had been carrying deep in the muscles of her shoulders and back eased a bit. "Thank you for doing this. The kids really need some downtime, just to sit around and watch TV, maybe make some cookies, even if it's just for a few days."

"It seems like you could use some of that, too."

Jo blew out air. "As soon as I'm able. I'm sorry about your trip."

"There'll be other trips." She waved her hand. "Sloan filled me in a bit. Hopefully you can find what you need more easily without the children tagging along."

"I'm not used to being without them." Jo sat on the edge of the bed. "Even after David and I split up, he'd only take them for the day. They spent every single night under my roof with me."

Evelyn sat beside her. "Every night?"

"Except for the occasional sleepover at a friend's house for April." She hung her head. "Stupid to get upset about it."

Evelyn's arm came around her shoulders. "Oh, it's not stupid at all. I remember when Sloan was little, I refused to let his father put him in his crib at bedtime. I wanted him next to me. That boy slept in a bassinet until he couldn't fit in it anymore." She stroked Jo's hair. "I'll bet you're a wonderful mother."

How many times had this woman acted as a mother to her? Jo's own mom had died when Jo was four. She had only a handful of memories of her, and none of them distinct. But Evelyn had been different, forever offering up her sound advice and comfortable shoulder whenever Jo had needed it. "April hates me. Lucas misses his father, and I have no idea what to do with that."

"And Fiona?"

"She loves me, but give her time."

Evelyn chuckled. "That sounds about par for the course. Just keep your chin up and know, the one thing they'll remember most is love."

Jo sat upright and wiped her nose. "Thanks, Ev. I really appreciate the pep talk."

"Cut yourself some slack. I imagine it can't be easy to be around my son, either."

Jo bit her lip, needing to talk honestly with this woman, yet unsure if she should. "Did Sloan tell you I asked him to marry me before he went in the Navy?"

"He did."

"He wouldn't do it. I didn't understand why, and I was so hurt and angry."

"He was devastated when you two broke up. And when he found out you'd married David... well, let's just say it wasn't pretty. He's never been quite the same, you know. He's different when you're around. I was watching him talking with you in the RV, and I think it was the first time I've seen him truly happy in a very long time."

"We were fighting."

"He's happy."

"He wants to take me to dinner."

"And what do you want to do?"

"Say yes." She looked at her hands. "But the kids already like him too much, and I'm afraid they'll get attached."

"Would that be so bad?"

"If things didn't go well between me and Sloan, yes. They just lost their father."

"And you don't want to risk it."

"That's right."

Evelyn took her hand. "Risk is what makes life worth living."

"Risk gives me panic attacks."

The older woman laughed. "I'm being serious, Jo. Every good thing can only enter your life if you're willing to shake things up a little. Otherwise, your life will never change."

"But the kids need stability."

"And love. It's clear to me they have yours in spades, but

if they'll ever have it from another parent, you will have to open that gate."

"He's only been gone a few days!"

"And if you were in mourning, I would bow my head and weep with you, sweetheart. But you're not. You aren't holding that gate closed with all your might because you just lost your love. You're holding it closed to keep love out. And that's something I just can't abide."

Joanne pulled her hand back. "It's not that simple."

"Isn't it? Or are you making it more complicated than it has to be?" Evelyn stood and picked up a folded blanket from a chair. "Now move your tuchus so I can finish making this bed."

This woman should have been a lawyer. She could peel back the layers on any argument, exposing the hard truth beneath. "He broke my heart."

"Ah, now we're getting somewhere. Up."

Jo stood and moved to the other side of the bed to help. "And I'm scared he's going to do it again."

Evelyn spread out the blanket over the bed. "He might. But you'll never know without trying. And he just might be the best thing to ever happen to those kids." She smiled. "I should get dinner started so you two can eat before you get back on the road. That's if I really can't convince you to stay the night."

"There isn't enough room. Besides, Sloan wanted to get a look at the warehouse tonight while no one's there."

"A big old warehouse on the river, at night. Sounds terrifying."

Joanne nodded. But the clock was ticking on Bannon's invisible timer, counting down to incalculable danger that put the lives of her children in jeopardy. She took a shaking breath in. "For more reasons than one."

20

It was blustery and dark, a cold wind blowing in gusts across the empty parking lot of Poughkeepsie Plumbing Supply. A chain-link fence surrounded the property, train tracks running between the warehouse and the Hudson River some forty feet away. The fence was buckled in places, wood pallets stacked up behind the building like discarded gift boxes on Christmas morning. A small addition stuck out from the side of the main building like a metal-roofed shanty.

Sloan used his banged-up NVGs to scope out the telephone poles and tall buildings around the property, Joanne on his heels.

"Are you sure we shouldn't wait until HERO Force gets here tomorrow?" she asked.

"I just want to check it out. See if we can get the lay of the land while no one's around."

"What exactly are we looking for?"

"Security cameras, for starters. Doesn't look like they have any."

"I'd think they would have put their money into

repaving this parking lot before they'd do anything high-tech, don't you?"

He moved toward a particularly badly buckled section of fencing farthest away from the light. "Let's get in there and take a look around." He stepped aside for her to go first. "You remember how to climb a fence?"

"It's four feet tall, Sloan. I think I can manage."

A light breeze carried the scent of fried food from a restaurant nearby, and he moaned. "You know what I love? Fried dough with powdered sugar. Food of the gods."

She took one big step up the fence, then threw her leg over the top. "Do you ever stop thinking about food?"

"No." He made it over the fence in one practiced movement. "Oh, with honey on top. Hell yeah. I gotta make me some of that when I get home." He moved toward the door to the shanty, which, upon closer inspection, appeared to be an office.

"What if there's an alarm?"

"Then we run very, very fast. Come on." He stopped at the door, finding it locked, and unzipped his rucksack.

"What are you looking for?"

"Lock-picking tools."

"You just carry those around?"

"Only when I'm going to be picking locks." It was a complicated mechanism, but well within his skill. He eyed Joanne as he worked. "What were you and my mom talking about back at the cabin?"

"Nothing."

"You can just say you don't want to tell me."

"Fine. I don't want to tell you."

"Hmm. Must have been good."

She didn't answer.

Really must have been good.

He'd been walking by the door and heard his name, barely resisting the urge to stop and listen. He would have paid money to be a fly on the wall for that conversation. Jo and his mom had always had a good relationship, which was far easier to accept when he and Jo had a good one of their own.

The lock clicked. "Got it. Come on."

He shined the light on the room around them, illuminating a desk, several filing cabinets, and two tables full of plumbing parts. He felt Jo walking behind him in the darkness, hating how aware he was of her presence.

Did she feel it, too? This thread that joined them like an electrical wire, its current surging? It was worse now that her kids were gone, even worse still as his adrenaline surged, anticipating a possible showdown tomorrow. He was drawn to that current, desperate to touch it, no matter that he would be burned.

And he would be burned—of that, he was certain. If not by the intensity of their connection, then by the opening of that same old wound from when she left.

The thought brought him up short. He'd been so damn angry when she married Regan that anger was his predominant emotion. But there had been a wound beyond his temper, a hurt he realized now he'd never been able to fix.

"You check the filing cabinet. I'll check the desk," he said, pulling a second flashlight from his pack and handing it to her. A train whistle sounded in the distance, a low vibration growing as the locomotive got closer.

Most of the drawers were full of office supplies, but one had a checkbook. He flipped through the duplicate copies, finding nothing unexpected for a plumbing supply company. He threw it back in the drawer.

"I found bank account statements," said Jo. "A bunch of them."

"How much money?"

"A lot more than you'd need to fix that parking lot and install some cameras. Seven figures."

Suddenly, bright light streamed in from windows on either side of the room. "Shit. Give me those." He took the files from her hand and stuffed them into his pack.

"What do we do?"

"Come. Follow me." He crouched down low and opened the door, the distant barking of a dog immediately catching his attention. He hadn't heard a dog the whole time they'd been on the property. The paths that had been dark were now lit by bright sodium lights.

Shit.

Turning away, he raced for the fence. That dog definitely seemed to be getting closer. They'd obviously tripped some kind of alarm or had been otherwise discovered. He reached the fence, but here thick brush grew through it and over it, making it difficult to scale.

The train whistle blew again and the train passed by, the rumbling drowning out all other sounds, though he knew the animal was there. He cursed into the din, running along the back of the building toward a small clearing in the brush, looking over his shoulder to be sure Joanne was there. She was, but behind her, the shape of the charging dog could be seen heading straight toward them.

He ran as fast as he could, reaching the clearing and hopping the fence with his good arm, then turned to help Joanne over it as well. She had one foot up high in the chain links when the dog caught up to her, barking wildly and attaching to her other foot.

He saw the fear in her eyes and watched her mouth form

his name, but he couldn't hear her scream over the sound of the train. He was already reaching for her, desperate to pull her over the fence, but his prosthetic arm couldn't lift her weight. He climbed onto the fence, bending over it to get a better grip around her body with his good arm, and heaved her over the top. They landed hard, him on his back and her on top of him, and scrambled to their feet as the train finally passed the warehouse and the sound waned.

Sloan's prosthesis had been pulled off his body and was hanging from its strap. Without it, his rucksack shifted awkwardly from his other shoulder. "Come on!" he demanded, forcing her into action.

"Your arm!"

"It's fine. Go!"

The sound of running footsteps followed them from inside as they raced along the fence back to the car. Sloan threw his prosthesis in the back and peeled away from the curb, taking off down the street.

21

———

Jo was shaking, blood streaming down her calf and onto her tennis shoe, but it was the image of Sloan's arm dangling from its socket that terrorized her.

She knew it was a prosthesis, but with it on, at least he looked whole. Once it was off, she could no longer pretend he wasn't broken, that everything about him was the same as it always had been.

"Are you okay?" he asked. "How bad did he get you?"

"I don't know. I can't see it."

"I'll pull over as soon as I can." He was swerving through the wet streets, snow having changed to rain that now fell heavily as he passed slower cars and flew up an expressway ramp. "Just need to make sure we lost them. Thank God we got rid of the Winnebago."

He accelerated on the highway, and she closed her eyes against a wave of nausea, keeping them that way for several minutes until she felt him descend on the curving exit ramp. "I think we're safe," he said. A hotel sign shone down the street, and he pulled into the parking lot. "No one followed us off the expressway." He turned the interior light on. "Let me see your foot."

She lifted her leg, bending it over the center console. "It's more like my calf and ankle."

He pulled it toward him, turning it slowly in the light, blood everywhere. "I have some first aid supplies in my pack, but I'd rather clean it out in the room so I can get a good look at the damage."

She nodded, pulling her leg back to her side of the car as he drove to the hotel, parked, and went inside to check in. He emerged several minutes later, grabbed his rucksack and prosthetic, and nodded toward her bag. "I can't carry any more right now."

"Oh, right," she said awkwardly, hyperconscious of his missing arm. "It's no problem. I've got it." She followed him through the hotel.

"I got adjoining rooms. Come in and let me take a look at that leg." He opened the door and held it for her to enter. "Why don't you sit on the edge of the bathtub?"

"Sure." She sat down and peeled off her bloody tennis shoe. A moment later, Sloan entered, dropping his rucksack on the ground. He was shirtless, with his prosthetic arm now reattached and a leather strap holding it in place.

Sweet mother of God.

His chest was more muscular than it had been when they were kids, a light dusting of dark hair accentuating his defined pecs and abs before disappearing at the waistband of his jeans. He was stocky and solid; every inch of him was pure, strong man. She swallowed against the dryness in her throat as he grabbed a cup off the sink and sat beside her on the edge of the tub.

He smelled spicy and male, the scent instantly registering on her senses like an alarm piercing the air. He turned on the water, waited for it to warm up, then filled the cup and rinsed away the blood a little at a time. "Does that hurt?"

"No."

He reached for a towel and placed it over his thigh before picking up her leg and gently placing it across his lap. He patted it dry with the towel, several gashes and a deep gouge marring her skin. His thumb slid along the sensitive flesh beside her injuries, and she sucked in a breath at his touch.

He did it again, his gaze fixed on the bites. "I almost didn't get you out of there in time."

"But you did."

He shot her a harsh look before reaching for his pack. "Barely." He took out bandages and first aid cream.

"Sloan, if it hadn't been for you, I would have been dog food."

He applied cream to the bandages and carefully placed them on the wounds. "My damn arm fell off."

"So what?"

"Don't patronize me, Jo."

"Patronize you how? You saved me. You pulled me over the fence and saved me from that dog."

"These wounds are deep. Another minute and who knows what that animal might have done?"

"But he didn't—"

"Stop pretending it doesn't matter that I fucked up, okay? Stop acting like you didn't notice that it almost got you killed." Finished with her bandages, he put her leg down and stood. "I was there. I know exactly what happened."

She followed him out of the bathroom. "So, let me get this straight. In your mind, you nearly got me killed because you were injured fighting for our country and that somehow makes you a bad person who can't be trusted with my care."

He'd walked away from her and now stood gazing out the window, his body silhouetted against the pane, hands on his hips. "I thought I could make a difference working for HERO Force."

She cocked her head, desperate to keep up with this change in conversation. She approached him. "Go on."

"I thought it wouldn't matter that I only had one arm. I had a good prosthetic. I could fire a gun. I could still fight the bad guys and come back begging for more." He shook his head. "But it isn't true."

"A few dog bites, and you're questioning your choice of career?"

"It's not the first time. I was down in Mexico on a mission. Damn near got my friend and two innocent civilians killed for the same reason. I was lucky I didn't hurt anyone else like I almost did today."

His pain was palpable, and she longed to take it away, absolve him of this sin he clearly hadn't committed. She reached out and tentatively laid her hand on his back. "I'll bet you helped them."

He turned around quickly, brushing off her hand in the process. "No, Jo. This story doesn't have a happy ending. I've been struggling for a long time, hiding behind a joke and pretending I fit in with the other guys. Hell, I think I was struggling even before that. First I lost you, then I lost the SEALs. I didn't think I could lose anything I loved again."

In that moment, she needed to soothe his pain just as he'd soothed hers. She closed the distance between them, going up on tiptoe to take his mouth in a kiss that conveyed every bit of passion she was feeling in her heart. He hesitated, and she feared he'd pull back. Her arms snaked up his chest to hold him to her, her lips and tongue demanding he respond.

Damn it, I know you remember how good we could be together. Show me. Show me you remember.

This was what she wanted, she could see so clearly now. Gone were her fears of being hurt by him again. She was already hurting, and she would go on hurting. She might as well enjoy him while she could.

His good arm came around her waist, holding her there, and his prosthetic did the same on the other side. She was hyperaware he couldn't feel anything with that limb, and she desperately wanted him to feel every inch of her body with every inch of her own. "Can I take this off?"

He leaned back, breaking their kiss. "Why?"

"It isn't you. I want to feel you."

He set her aside. "It's part of me now."

"No, I just meant..." Her voice trailed off. She could see she'd made a horrible mistake, only intensifying his emotional moment. "I'm sorry." She closed the distance between them and touched his chest lightly with her palm. "Please."

"Please, what?"

She swallowed against her discomfiture. "I want to kiss you." His expression told her he was angry, torn between taking her offer and walking away. She licked her lips. She had to try again. "Do you know how many times I've dreamed about kissing you? Being back in your arms, just one more time?"

"Arm. Singular."

"I don't care about that. You're still you. That's what I really wanted."

His eyes darkened, his gaze slipping down her face to her lips, hovering there. "I dreamed of you, too." His hand slipped into the hair at the nape of her neck, lifting her face to his. "But my dreams didn't stop at kissing."

Adrenaline surged into her bloodstream, a pulse beating between her legs. Memories of him swarmed like bees, from the first time he penetrated her, taking her virginity, to the desperation of teenage lust, searching for release.

His hand moved from her neck to her collarbone, trailing sensation as he traced the outline of her breast and moved lower. His big hand slid around her midriff and farther to cup her derriere.

Her eyelids grew heavy as he held her against his hardening erection, and she fitted her torso more completely against his, her arms coming to circle his neck as she kissed his jaw, his stubble abrading her lips.

Then he was kissing her, deep, demanding kisses that flooded all rational thought. There was only feeling, only emotion, only the desperate need to be as close to him as possible.

His hands slipped under her shirt, lifting it over her head in one smooth motion. His hand moved to her lace-covered breast, taking its fullness in his palm and kneading it before circling her nipple with his thumb.

Her back arched in response, thrusting her rib cage closer to him, and he pulled the cup of her bra down to expose her fully. She felt the warmth of his breath before he took her in his mouth, licking and suckling her deep.

She bucked wildly against him, desperate for these feelings only he could bring, and her nails dug into the flesh of his lower back. "Sloan," she said on a moan, needing him to know what he was doing to her, needing to connect with him even more than he was doing now.

His head came up and he kissed her, lifting her with his powerful arm and all but dragging her to the bed. He followed her down, the planes of his body accentuated by shadow, and she reached out to touch every inch of his flesh.

The scent of his body was heady and familiar as her hands raked over his chest. She bent to kiss his nipple, the taste of his salty skin further fanning her desire. She moved up to his neck, kissing him there as her hands reached down to unbutton his jeans.

"Jesus, Jo," he ground out under his breath, helping her get his pants off and shucking them down his legs.

He wore black briefs, his cock tenting the fabric, and her hands moved over it, outlining his sensitive shaft and cupping his balls before stroking them tenderly.

His breath caught, its rhythm faster now, and she longed to push him closer to the edge. Sliding her body down the bed, she kissed him through the fabric where her hands had been, loving how he cursed and twisted beneath her.

She hadn't given oral sex in years, hadn't wanted to, but now she was as desperate to taste him as she was to receive his attention. Slipping her hand beneath the material, she fisted her fingers around his firm shaft and breathed heavily on the fabric-covered tip. "God, yes," he ground out, and she pulled down the waistband, exposing him completely.

His cock was glorious, thick and wide, and she licked the bulbous head before taking him in her mouth, instantly remembering what he liked. She teased him, sinking onto him slowly before taking as much as she could and loving every groan and hiss of his reaction.

Then he was pulling her up, wrestling her onto her back and assaulting her with a sensual attack. His mouth was back on her breast while his hand moved down to skillfully stroke the sensitive seam of her sex. Her legs fell open at his touch, hungry for more.

His stubble lightly abraded her abdomen as he moved

lower, reverently kissing her skin until he reached the inside of her thigh and stopped. "So beautiful," he whispered, his fingers tracing her swollen lips before slowly slipping deep inside her.

She bucked against the mattress. Then his tongue was on her clitoris, a wave of sensation building as his fingers moved to the rhythm of his mouth.

No one else had loved her like this. No one had tasted and touched as if he were receiving a precious gift, and she longed to hold him inside her and never let go. "Please," she begged, not wanting to reach orgasm without him. "I need you now."

He rolled onto his back beside her and she straddled him, experiencing only a flash of concern as she sank down on his bare shaft. She thought of the condom in his wallet. They had never used one before, but she'd been on the pill back when they'd been dating. She wasn't on the pill now.

He filled her completely, and it felt so deliciously good she couldn't bear the thought of stopping. It was lunacy and she knew it, consequences be damned.

His hands moved to her waist and she instinctively jerked away from his cold prosthetic, but he held her there, moving her hips onto him as he thrust beneath her.

She was frantic now, her body racing toward release, and she pumped as quickly as she could until the orgasm came, unable to move in the moment.

He flipped her over, bracing himself on his good arm as he drove into her again and again, finally joining her in sexual oblivion.

22

———————

Sloan stared at the ceiling, Joanne sleeping soundly on his shoulder as he absently stroked her skin. He'd slept for a few hours but had woken shortly before four, unable to get back to sleep.

He was blown away.

He'd slept with plenty of women since this one, but none of them compared. It wasn't a physical comparison but a spiritual one. He hadn't been as connected to any of them as he'd always been to Joanne, and that was a problem.

Making love to her was like picking up where they'd left off years before, and he was suddenly concerned with all the reasons he'd dropped out of that race in the first place. Jo had changed the rules on him halfway around the track, asking him to marry her and take her away from her abusive father forever.

She'd been asking him to save her.

He'd been a stupid kid back then, just barely eighteen and on his way into the military. He had nothing to offer her but himself. That wasn't how love was supposed to manifest, like some kind of dare that seemed like a super-bad idea.

Now he'd gone and made love to her without a condom.
Speaking of super-bad ideas.

It wasn't like it had slipped his mind. He always practiced safe sex and had a condom in his wallet right now. But he hadn't used it, needing to feel every part of the experience just as he had felt it back then. Condoms were for other relationships, not for this one.

Fuck.

Worse yet, in that moment, he'd considered the possibility of her getting pregnant, and the idea only increased his desire to make love without one.

What was he looking for here? Joanne was back in his life and looking for him to save her again. It's not like she'd come looking for him to give their relationship another try. She'd shown up on his doorstep desperate for help, and he knew in his heart she wouldn't otherwise have been there.

To make matters worse, he was getting attached. Not just to Jo but also to the kids. She'd asked him not to be nice to them for their own sake, but he should have been more concerned with saving himself. Instead, he hadn't given it a care.

Lucas was a trip, reminding Sloan of himself at that age. And Fiona, well, the devil himself would fall in love with that girl. April was at a tough age, but she had a good head on her shoulders and her mother's big heart.

He kissed the top of Jo's head. There was no way this was going to end well for him. He'd help her find the money and get to a safe place with her kids. Then he would have to get over her all over again. Wouldn't be the first time he'd learned to live without her, but this time he swore would be the last.

He opened his eyes. He needed sleep, but it wasn't likely to come as he battled regrets and poor decisions. After slipping his arm out from beneath her neck and quietly getting out of bed, he grabbed the files they'd taken from the plumbing supply company and headed into the adjoining room. If he was going to be awake, he might as well do something useful.

He clicked on the light and got to work, inspecting each account and making notes on when deposits were made. Most of the money was moved in the past three months— more than ninety percent of it—and all of it in amounts less than three thousand dollars. Perhaps a larger transfer would have attracted attention.

All totaled, there was just over two-point-two million. But was it their missing money? If David had taken it and given it to his mistress, she could well be hiding it here. Moto would have to go through the transactions and follow the trail to confirm, but it sure looked like they'd found what they'd been looking for. Only question now was, would Bannon accept that his wife, McKenzie, was involved? They would need proof—that much was sure.

He dialed Moto, who answered on the first ring despite the hour. "What's up?"

Sloan told him about the account activity he needed traced. "I'll email you scans of the account information."

"So nobody's dead or dying right now?"

"Nope."

"Then why the fuck are you calling me at four a.m.?"

Sloan grinned. "Figured you'd be easy to get ahold of."

"I spent my day riding a horse."

"You don't strike me as the ranch-hand type."

"I'm not, and you damn well know it. I can't fucking move, and my ass feels like its been pounded with two-by-fours for hours."

"Look at you with the Home Depot reference. You keep this up, Moto, you just might earn that man card back."

"Fuck you, Dvorak. I'm going to sleep."

"All right. Just get me bank info as soon as you can."

"Got it."

Sloan grinned. Mac O'Brady had one hell of a sense of humor, sending Moto to a horse farm in Wyoming like that, even with Trace there to help him blend in.

He stood and began to pace, running a hand through his hair. He was stressed. Uncomfortable. Something was bothering him, and he tried to place his discomfort. He was knee deep in the throes of relationship hell with Joanne, that was certain. But something about this money scheme and the visit to the warehouse tonight was all wrong.

It was too easy.

From the moment they'd set their sights on coming here, his gut had been telling him this would be a dangerous mission. And while the dog had been alarming, it was not the battle his subconscious had been anticipating.

Maybe he'd been wrong, and there was nothing here to fear. Or maybe they'd only scratched the tip of the iceberg, and the *Titanic* was about to go down.

He plopped down on the bed and closed his eyes, letting his mind wander. His last coherent thought was that he should have been with Joanne in the next room, as fatigue abruptly overtook the last vestiges of consciousness.

23

Joanne awoke from a deep sleep feeling more rested than she had in weeks. She opened her eyes. Making love to Sloan came back to her in a rush of heated memory, along with what they needed to do today. In an instant, her anxiety was back.

Where was Sloan?

She sat up, making her way to the heavy drapes and opening them to a dark and rainy day. That didn't bode well. The door to the adjoining room was open, and she crossed to it. "Sloan?" The bathroom door was closed and she could hear the shower running. The bed had clearly been slept in, and she frowned, not knowing what to make of that.

The files from the plumbing supply company were spread out on the desk. He must have come in here to work, or else he was having second thoughts about last night and wanted to put as much distance between them as possible. She wasn't sure she wanted to know which.

She needed to find her Rolaids. Returning to her room, she dialed Evelyn's cell phone. Fiona answered. "Hi, Mom. We made rainbow pancakes with sprinkles!"

"Wow, it sounds like you're having fun."

"Mmm-hmm. Miss Evelyn's going to draw with me next. She's playing poker with Lucas."

"Poker, huh?"

"Yeah. We did Crazy Eights first. I won thirty-eight cents."

Of course they were betting for money. "That's awesome, sweetie. Can I talk to Evelyn for a minute?"

She got on the phone. "How's it going down there?"

"So far, so good. We found some records I hope will point us in the right direction. How are the kids?"

"Lucas and Fiona are good. April spent last night moping around the house. Something about a boy you won't let her talk to."

Jo pinched the skin between her eyes. "Can I talk to her?"

"She isn't awake yet. Nothing surer to drive two lovebirds together than to forbid them from seeing each other."

"Ev, she doesn't even know this boy! She met him online. What if he's a stalker, or a predator of some kind? She invited him to our campsite in Chicago without asking me and Sloan nearly shot the poor guy."

"Good lord."

It occurred to her April might have reinstalled the same app. She hated to be so suspicious of her own daughter, but that didn't mean she wasn't. "Can you do me a favor?" She walked Evelyn through how to search for Instagram on April's phone.

"Nope, no Instagram."

Jo exhaled and dropped her shoulders. "Thank God. Let's hope it stays that way."

"Should I wake her up or just let her sleep?"

She looked at the clock, surprised to see it was already

almost ten. "Let her sleep another thirty minutes or so, then you can wake her up. Thanks, Ev."

She hung up just as Sloan walked into the room with only a towel slung around his waist, the smell of soap surrounding him. His prosthetic was once again in place.

"You ever take that thing off around women?"

"All the time."

She really didn't like that answer, especially coupled with her insecurities over him sleeping in the next room. "I'm going in the shower."

She washed her body with hotter-than-hot water, wishing she'd been blessed with mind-reading abilities so she knew what that man was thinking. The men of HERO Force would be arriving soon, precluding further private conversation, and she wanted to know where she stood.

"I'm not sorry," she whispered under her breath. "I will never be sorry." No matter what happened from here on out, she'd followed her heart and opened herself up to Sloan. That was an accomplishment, not something to be ashamed of or worried about.

When she dried off, she removed her bandages and winced. That didn't look good at all, and she cleaned it carefully before putting on a new bandage. She dressed quickly in the hot, steamy bathroom, wishing she could go in the cooler bedroom but too confused about her standing with Sloan to walk in there nearly naked, as he had done. The thought further frustrated her already frazzled nerves, and she was thoroughly hot and cranky by the time she emerged.

Once again, Sloan wasn't there, which irritated her that much more. She tied her hair back in a ponytail and went in search of him, finding him at the desk in the adjoining room, on the phone. He held up a finger.

"I really appreciate you doing this so quickly, Moto. I'll be in touch." He hung up. "You're not going to believe this. All of these accounts have been emptied in the past eight days."

"All of them?"

"Every last one, all two-point-two million dollars and change."

"Our missing money. Where did it go?"

"An account in the Cayman Islands." His phone vibrated, and he looked at the screen. "Mac and Champion are on their way up. You ready to find McKenzie?"

The moment was slipping right out of reach, and she needed to get it back. She'd go crazy if they didn't talk about the elephant in the room before leaving here. "Actually, I was hoping we could talk for a minute."

"Shoot." His phone rang. "Hang on, it's my mom again. Hello?"

He shot panicky eyes to hers as he listened to the phone. "What do you mean?"

Joanne could hear Evelyn's voice rising and falling with emotion. "What happened?" she whispered.

"April's not in her room."

"*What?* Put her on speaker."

He hit a button. "...woods around the cabin, but I don't see her. Should I call the police?"

Jo was light-headed with fear. "Did she leave on her own? Was anyone there?"

"As far as I knew, everything was fine. I went upstairs to wake her like you asked me to, and it doesn't even look like her bed was slept in last night."

"Did she run away?" Jo clutched at his shirt. "Was she that mad at me? We have to find her. We have to find her, Sloan!"

"I should have had guys stationed at the cabin," he barked. "Damn it, I thought she'd be safe. Call the police. I'll get HERO Force out there as soon as I can. I'll call you back." He hung up.

"He couldn't have found the kids. He couldn't have!" She was losing it, the panic attack appearing out of nowhere and instantly on overdrive.

He held her by her upper arms. "Listen to me. She's a smart kid. She wouldn't have run away in the middle of winter in a place she doesn't know."

She swallowed against the knot in her throat, knowing he was right but unable to comprehend the consequences of the truth. "Then she was taken. But how? This doesn't make any sense! We checked every device, everything. We were careful."

"It's like they had inside information. Someone telling them where we were."

"But who would do that? The kids know we're in danger. They wouldn't be so foolish as to tell someone where they are." An image of April in tears at the campground appeared in her mind. "No..."

"What is it?"

"It's not possible." She ran to the other room and picked up her phone, searching for Instagram and downloading the app, Sloan entering the room behind her. "The guy on Instagram who had me so concerned. I just assumed he was a kid, but what if he's not?"

"What do you mean?"

"What if he's Bannon, or one of his guys? All you need to fake an identity on Instagram is a profile picture." The possibilities were horrible and endless. "But your mom checked for me last night. April hadn't reinstalled the app."

"I saw her on Fiona's iPad." He headed for the other room. "I'm calling my mother back."

The app finished downloading and Jo opened it. She knew April's email address but not her password. She tried the one she used for everything, knowing the kids often did the same. "Please, God, let this work…" The screen changed to April's feed. "I'm in!"

A knock sounded on the bedroom door. "I got it. That's Mac," called Sloan. "Mom, I need you to check Fiona's iPad. See if she has Instagram."

Jo found her way to April's messages as Sloan greeted the men. The messages came one after another from Justin971—the most recent posting at eleven o'clock last night.

I'll meet you by the main road.

"No, no, no…" she whispered, scrolling to read their earlier conversation.

Sloan swore loudly. "She had Instagram on the iPad."

"I know. I'm in her account. She was talking to him."

This stupid log cabin. I have to share a room with my sister…

That sucks. Where are you?

The thriving metropolis of Esopus, New York.

I'm visiting my aunt in New York City. That's not too far away. With your mom gone, we could see each other. I'll take an Uber like last time.

Isn't that expensive?

It would be worth it to see you.

Okay, that would be great! I'm at 818 Creek Road.

"Jesus Christ, she gave him the address." She stood and raised her voice to be heard over the men, who'd grown louder as Sloan filled them in. "She gave him her address!" The phone vibrated in her hand. She had a new text from a number she didn't recognize, and she opened it.

TIME'S UP.

I'VE GOT THE GIRL, NOW I WANT MY MONEY.

LEAVE IT ON THE BENCH BY THE STATUE AT JEFFERSON PARK AT 10:00 P.M. COME ALONE.

I'LL CONTACT YOU AFTER.

24

———

Sloan knew this had been too easy.

His gut was never wrong, and this mission had just taken a serious turn for the worse, with April's life hanging in the balance. Rage twisted with protective-ness, his blood pumping fast. She wasn't his flesh-and-blood child, but she could have been, and that made every differ-ence in his heart.

"We don't even have the money!" Joanne was hyperventi-lating, clearly having a panic attack, and he worried about her ability to handle this latest development. "How can we give them what we don't even have?"

He crossed to her and pulled her to a seated position on the bed. "Put your head between your knees. Take slow, even breaths." She did as he said.

"Gavin and Asher are in a chopper on their way here," said Mac, typing into his phone. "I'll reroute them to Wise-man's cabin to protect your family."

As much as Sloan wanted them protected, he was keenly aware they had limited resources and the need for men here. "We're going to need them. Get Evelyn and the kids to a safe location—without any of their damn devices—then I want Gavin and Asher back."

If there was one thing he hated, it was not knowing what he was up against. That could easily lead to the team being overpowered and a terrible outcome for April. He could hardly stand to think about it. He looked pointedly at Mac. "Who else can you spare?"

"Chop and Razorback."

Sloan cursed under his breath. It wasn't enough. "We have to win this one, Mac."

"I know." The older man nodded sagely, as if he could see how important this mission was to him personally. "I'll call Trace and Moto back from Wyoming. They should be able to make it in time."

Joanne slowly sat up, her hand clutching his arm. She looked utterly shaken. "What if McKenzie won't give us the money?"

"Then we fake it," said Mac. "Use dummy bills, make the drop, and get your daughter back. We've done it before. Just don't tell the US Marshals office."

Sloan nodded. "It won't fool them for long, but it could buy us crucial minutes to get April and get the hell out of there." He touched her back lightly. "Are you able to walk? We need to get to the warehouse and find McKenzie."

"Yes." She stood, her legs visibly trembling. "Just let me grab my phone."

Sloan crossed to Mac, lowering his voice. "I've got a bad feeling about this McKenzie character. She's Joanne's dead husband's lover."

Mac nodded. "Champ and I will stay on your six."

They drove to the warehouse in the HERO Force SUV, arriving just after noon. In the light of day, the river gleamed a foreboding gray, whitecaps on the surface from the heavy wind. The building itself was made of brick, a faded sign painted across the windowless facade reading POUGH-KEEPSIE PLUMBING SUPPLY.

Sloan convinced Joanne to wait in the car while he, Mac, and Champion headed for the office they'd investigated last night. This time he carried pepper spray, a weapon for an animal that might or might not appear, and wore the same pack on his back that he had last night.

He knew something was wrong as soon as he saw the office door standing slightly ajar. He drew his weapon, the other men doing the same. When he reached the entrance, he stood to the side before kicking it open with one leg and moving into the doorframe.

Everything was gone. Every paper, everything that had been on the desks and shelves except the plumbing parts on the tables. He carefully moved inside, clearing the room as he went, and opened the filing cabinet where they'd hit pay dirt last night. It, too, was empty. "Son of a bitch." He ran a hand through his hair. McKenzie had gotten wind of their visit last night and was gone.

"This was all full of paperwork. Records, that sort of thing." He sighed heavily. "Let's check the warehouse. We never made it in there last night."

He drew his weapon, again holding it at the ready. There were two weathered metal doors that seemed to lead to that area. It was dark inside and the glass dirty, making it impossible to see into the warehouse without going in.

The door squeaked loudly as he pulled it open, the combination of mold and rust assaulting his nose. It was dark, dank, and very cold, making him wonder if the heat was turned on at all. He pulled a flashlight from his pack as Mac and Champion did the same.

Row upon row of tall industrial racks filled the space,

boxes on more than half of them. Near the ceiling, a catwalk encircled the entire warehouse, a long walkway bisecting the space to connect the two sides. The sound of running water came from deeper in the building, and Sloan followed it, looking for the source.

Halfway down an exterior wall, a series of old metal pipes ran from the ceiling to the floor, an ice sculpture forming where one of them had burst. He followed the flow of water to an open grate, a throwback to a time when virtually anything could be connected to the public sewer system directly.

"There's nobody here," he said, his voice echoing in the space. "McKenzie probably saw us come in last night and figured she'd clear out of Dodge. We're going to have to get April back the hard way."

"We can handle it, Dvorak. We've got the men."

Sloan shook his head as he turned and walked past them. "I goddamn knew this wasn't going to be easy."

25

———

There was no snow tonight, the bright light of the moon throwing everything into relief. Jefferson Park sat in the middle of downtown Poughkeepsie, a wide space containing a playground, basketball court, picnic area, and a small amphitheater showcasing local graffiti. The entire park was surrounded by buildings, including the library and courthouse, though this part of downtown was deserted at night.

At its center stood a statue of Thomas Jefferson, flanked by a park bench and a large black garbage can. That was where the drop was to be made. Joanne had been told to come by herself. If any of the men could have passed for her size and physique, they would have gone instead, but in the end, it needed to be her, leaving Sloan terrified he could end up with both her and April being gone—or worse.

Sloan and Moto were positioned in the library with a prime view of the statue, Champion on the roof with a high-powered sniper rifle. Mac and Trace were in the courthouse, Chop and Razorback in a van parked close to the basketball court, and Gavin and Asher each stationed farther out at either end of the park.

Chop and Razorback had been surveilling the area for nearly nine hours but had yet to see anyone who could be Bannon or one of his associates, much less Joanne's daughter.

Sloan checked his watch. Nine fifty-four. Any second now, a series of events would be set in motion, the final outcome still unknown, and the tension was eating him alive. It occurred to him he had more to lose tonight than he'd ever called his own, and he said a silent prayer for help. Champion's voice came over the comm set in his ear. "Here comes Jo."

He opened his eyes. She was walking up one of the sidewalks that went out from the statue like bicycle spokes, the shade of mature trees hiding her form before she emerged once more into the moonlight. He lifted his binoculars to his eyes. He could hear her breathing, the anxiety she so barely held under control. Her voice was a whisper in his ear. "I don't see anyone."

"Don't talk," snapped Sloan. "You can't let them see your mouth moving. Just put the money on the bench and get out of there."

Mac spoke next. "I've got eyes on a dark minivan heading your way. One block out, east side of the park."

Sloan stared through the binoculars. "Get out of there, Jo." She appeared from the shadows walking quickly out of the park, and the invisible noose around his neck loosened a degree. He trained the binoculars down the road, the minivan approaching in the distance. "It's got tinted windows. Can you see inside, Champion?" The sharpshooter had a night vision scope on his rifle, which he hoped could see through the glass.

"Affirmative, but I don't see the girl. Got two male tangos in the front seat."

The van approached the center of the park, stopping just behind the van with Razorback and Chop inside. "Fuck," said Razorback. "I think we've been made."

"Hang tight," said Mac. "Wait 'em out. They might just be checking to see."

Minutes passed, the blood rushing in Sloan's ears as sweat formed on his brow. Joanne spoke on the comm set. "I got a text. It says, 'Come out here.'"

"Shit," bit out Mac.

"I'm going," said Jo.

"No!" barked Sloan. "Stay where you are. They're on to us with the van. They could use you as a hostage to tie our hands."

"I'm telling them I want to see April."

She was thinking about doing it, putting herself directly in harm's way to save her child, rendering HERO Force defenseless against an attack. "Jo, we'll move the van. Stay put."

The side of the minivan slid open. Joanne gasped. "She's tied up on the floor."

"Affirmative," said Champion. "I have a visual on the girl."

"They say for me to come to the van. I'm going out there."

"Damn it, Jo, no!" But he was too late, Joanne already moving quickly onto the scene. Just as he feared, the passenger-side door opened, a figure in black holding a gun trained directly on Jo. She raised her hands, unmoving.

They only had a moment before she became his hostage. Sloan saw the slightest window of opportunity. "Champ, can you get a shot?"

"Negative. The girl's too close to the tango from this angle."

"Goddamn it!" Sloan watched in horror as the man in black crossed to Jo, wrapping one arm around her neck and using her body to shield his own.

"Hold your fire!" shouted Mac. "We have a hostage situation. Stand down. Gavin and Asher, move to the southern entrance to the park. Now!"

Sloan ran for the library door, drawing his Sig Sauer, Moto on his heels. He exited the building and hopped the railing, landing behind a hedgerow that hugged the foundation and hid him from view. He rounded the corner of the building and crouched low in the plants.

The man had pulled Joanne to the bench and taken the money and was making his way back to the minivan. "It's all there, I promise you," Jo said, and Sloan filled with fear the tangos would find her comm set.

"And you promised to come alone," said the man. "Your word is no good."

"Just let her go. My daughter didn't do anything wrong."

The duo went into shadow then popped out again, Joanne clearly having a hard time walking with his arm around her neck. He was still holding her against his torso as he ordered, "Get in the van. You're my ticket out of this place."

"Don't do it," Sloan hissed. "Try to get away."

"I'll come with you if you let her go," Jo said.

Sloan wanted to scream at her not to do it, but knew his voice might be heard over the comm set in her ear if he did.

"What is this?" demanded the man.

Fear went through Sloan like an icy breeze. Had he found the comm set anyway?

"You stupid whore." The man pushed her into the

waiting minivan, following her in. "Give me that thing." The sound of the comm set in the man's hand was followed by the click of it hitting the pavement. The van door slid shut and the vehicle took off down the road, Sloan instantly on the run after it.

"Hit the tires," barked Mac, gunfire erupting on the scene from Champion's rifle.

Sloan was running as hard as he could, his horror causing time to stretch out like taffy. Those men had April, Joanne, and the counterfeit money. It was only a matter of time before they realized it wasn't real and took retaliatory action.

Sparks flew from the back hubcap and the minivan went hard right, kissing a tree before continuing on awkwardly. Sloan stopped running and aimed his weapon on the opposite tire, which deflated instantly. The vehicle all but stopped. Asher appeared some fifty feet away, preparing to cut off the van from the passenger side. Sloan positioned himself perpendicular to the van and trained his gun on the driver as Asher approached from the other side.

The passenger fired. Sloan did, too, putting several shots into the front seat of the vehicle but careful to avoid the back. Moto and Gavin arrived on the scene, quickly followed by Mac, each of them with the now-unmoving tangos now in their sights.

Sloan moved carefully to the sliding door and opened it, his weapon ready to fire. There on the floor was April, tied up and sobbing as Joanne untied her bindings. He checked the men in the front seat, finding them both dead—Bannon and a younger man. "Tangos down," said. He moved to the back and took April's tied ankles into his lap, cutting the ties with his tactical knife and a shaking hand. "Any injuries?" he asked, aware of the strange emotion-filled quality of his voice and the tears that streamed down her face.

She shook her head.

He gestured to the younger man. "Is that the guy from Instagram?"

She nodded, her face crumpling as she sobbed. "He has a big cut on his arm."

"You scared the hell out of me, April. Thank God you're all right."

"I'm sorry."

Joanne opened her arms and held her. Mac ushered the three of them out of the car as local law enforcement arrived on the scene, blue and red lights bouncing off Thomas Jefferson and the park.

With April and her mother settled together on a bench, Sloan walked back toward the library, dropped into a squat, and wept for the terrible things that could have happened that day. He cried for the loss of Joanne and for finding her again, for her children and the chance to be part of their lives, if only for a moment. Bannon was dead. They'd gotten him. Joanne and her kids would be safe from now on, and no matter what happened between Sloan and Jo, he would forever be grateful.

He wiped his face and stood, turning back to the chaos, and was startled to find a man silhouetted against the emergency lights. Sloan was hyperaware of his lack of a gun, having left his Sig Sauer with the police officer in charge. "Can I help you?" he asked.

"It isn't over." He took off his hood, his features just barely visible in the low light. "I wish for Joanne's sake it was."

There was something familiar about this man, his height, his build, his voice...

"Bannon was only the beginning. It's McKenzie you need to be worried about."

Suddenly, Sloan knew exactly who stood in front of him, and dread settled in his stomach like a heavy weight. "David fucking Regan. I was wondering when you would rise from the dead."

26

___

avid is alive.

Joanne rode in the backseat of Mac's SUV, her arms around April. Sloan had called her aside at the park and told her about David's appearance. "I had Gavin take him to the house."

"Where are Lucas and Fiona?"

"A hotel about fifteen minutes from there with my mom. I think we should wait until morning to get them. No reason to wake everyone."

She agreed. "What about April? I don't want her seeing her father. It will just upset her. At least not right now."

"Already taken care of."

It was raining again, and her eyes caught on streetlights and signs, absently staring into the night. Bannon was dead, her clothes and April's both splattered with blood, the image of Bannon's open skull not likely to leave her memory anytime soon.

That should have been the end of it, but David told Sloan it was just the beginning, and that made Joanne want to cry. What had she done to deserve this? What had the kids? All of their current strife was David's fault, David and his inability to keep his dick in his pants.

They made it back to Sloan's house and she ushered April up the stairs, helping her into the shower, then tucking her into bed. The girl was exhausted, asleep before her head hit the pillow. Jo showered, then picked up their bloody clothes and threw them in the trash.

She was overly aware of David's presence in the house, waiting, a migraine taking root in her temples as she made herself hot tea. Sloan appeared in the kitchen doorway. "Are you ready?"

"I guess so." She followed him to the study, and he knocked. The lock clicked and the door opened. She was holding her breath as she looked at the man she'd thought she buried standing in the entrance to Sloan's favorite room.

David tucked his hands into his pockets. "Hi, Jo."

She wanted to slap him, but she clenched her jaw and walked past, sitting in the leather club chair as the men took their seats. "You have a lot of explaining to do."

"I know." He sat on one end of a long matching couch, Sloan at the other. He leaned forward, bracing his elbows on his knees. "I don't know where to start."

"How about you start with why you faked your own death."

"I didn't mean for that to happen." He hung his head. "You know I was seeing McKenzie," he said sheepishly.

"Yes."

"We were going to run away together. Start a new life. I thought I loved her." He rested the heel of his hand on his forehead. "She'd signed a prenuptial agreement with Bannon and wouldn't get any money if they divorced, even though he was worth millions." He sighed heavily. "She talked me into it. I ran his accounts. I could skim off the top and make it happen pretty easily. Over the course of a year and half, I took two-point-three million dollars."

He stood and walked to the fireplace mantel, staring at pictures in frames as he spoke. "It was all set up. We were transferring the money into an account in the Cayman Islands, preparing to leave."

"And the children?" she asked.

"There was five hundred thousand set aside for child support. We both know they'd be better off without me."

How many times had she thought the same thing herself? But him coming to that conclusion on his own was just another mark against him. What kind of man would leave his children behind without another thought?

"I was selfish, Jo, okay? I wanted a new start. Since you left, when it was my day with the kids, it was always terrible. Always. April yelling at me, Lucas and me fighting, even Fiona would break down in tears. I sounded just like my old man, treating my own children like shit, and I hated myself for it. I don't know how to be a good father. I didn't realize how much you helped me until I was on my own."

The pain in his voice was her undoing. Her eyes burned, emotion welling up as he admitted to his failures as a parent. More than his treatment of her, it had been the way he handled the kids that made her desperate to get away from him. But seeing the devastation in his eyes, knowing how hard it must have been roused her sympathy. She spoke the simple truth. "They love you, David. You're their father."

He frowned harshly.

"Who died in the fire?" asked Sloan.

"We were almost ready to go. McKenzie told me to meet her at the hunting cabin—we met there sometimes—but her cousin Finbar showed up instead. He was a lowlife I'd met a couple of times at her place. He was forever going in and out of jail.

"The son of a bitch mocked me. He knew everything, details he could only have gotten from McKenzie. Said he was getting a cut of the money, and all he had to do was kill me."

Joanne remembered the dark brown casket, her desire to see what was inside. "So it was Finbar we buried in that cemetery."

"I had no choice. It was him or me. McKenzie double-crossed me. She used me to steal Bannon's money and put her name on it, then she wanted me gone."

"So why not go to the police?" asked Sloan. "If you killed him in self-defense, that's justifiable homicide."

"Do you think she would have stopped?" he asked incredulously. "Do you think she would have let me live once I knew what she'd done? I could turn her in to Bannon in a heartbeat. I was a liability."

He sat back down. "I shot Finbar, and I set the fire to hide the evidence. I never knew I could act that way, do those things." He shook his head. "I watched the hunting cabin burn. That's when I realized everyone would think it was me in that building. That I could still have a fresh start, even without McKenzie." His eyes searched hers. "It never occurred to me they'd come after you, that I was putting our kids in danger."

The frown was back, his chin puckering. "I never would have done anything to hurt you guys on purpose." His voice cracked and he seemed to collapse in on himself, the weight of his decisions crushing the man he'd once been.

Joanne stood and crossed to the couch, sitting and putting her arms around him, aware of Sloan just a few feet behind her. She needed to do this, needed to find some forgiveness in this space. David had been damaged by his father just as Joanne had been damaged by hers. He was no more capable of being a good parent than she was of leaving her own scars behind.

David's shoulders shook. Her mind flipped through the pages of her relationship with each of these men, the dynamic between her and Sloan crystalizing in her understanding. She'd been looking for someone to save her from her father's wrath, a hero to make the darkness go away. When she'd asked him to marry her, she wasn't doing it out of love, even though she loved him with her whole heart and soul. She'd been asking him to take on that role forever, to keep her safe and protected so she wouldn't have to be brave.

Her relationship with David hadn't stood a chance.

"I'm so sorry," he said into her ear. "For all of it. The cheating and the lies. The unhappy years."

"I'm sorry, too." She gently rubbed his back. "I was expecting you to fix my life instead of sharing it with me. No one can do that for anyone else."

"It wasn't your fault."

She hadn't been looking for forgiveness, but the words resonated with her in a way that few ever had. Her throat constricted. "It wasn't your fault, either." She could see it now, the elusive truth suddenly staring her in the face. "I blamed you for everything, right from the start, and I'm sorry." She squeezed him tightly, then let him go, standing and returning to her seat.

Sloan stood and crossed to the sideboard, the sound of liquid pouring the only noise in the room. He brought them each a scotch, then took his seat. "You said Bannon was only the beginning, that it was McKenzie we had to worry about."

David nodded. "After she tried to kill me, I wanted to

make sure she couldn't keep a dime of that money. I'd paid a king's ransom for new identities for the two of us. Passports. Her ticket out of the country, the bank account in the Caymans—everything's in her new name. I broke into her house and I stole back the passport."

Joanne's mouth dropped open. "The day of the funeral, someone broke into our house. It was a mess, drawers emptied everywhere, paintings taken down. It looked like they were looking for something. But McKenzie was at the service with Bannon. She couldn't have done it.."

"She could have had someone else do it, just like she had Finbar try to kill me."

"Where are the passports now?" asked Sloan.

"In the glove box of the Porsche in your driveway. As far as I know, McKenzie still thinks I'm dead. If she already had the house checked, I've got ten bucks she's looking for that car—and for you."

27

———————

Within an hour, Sloan had Razorback, Chop, Gavin, and Asher doing guard duty outside of his house and the Porsche hidden safely in the garage. David was sure he'd mentioned Sloan to McKenzie over the years, though he wasn't sure the other woman had remembered the story of Joanne's first love, much less put the pieces together and figured out they were staying here.

Sloan set David up on the couch to sleep. "It's not so bad if you put your head at the high end."

Joanne stood at the foot of the stairs. "You can sleep with me."

He nodded, unsure of whether she was offering him a comfortable spot to rest his head or the comfort of her body. Unable to reject either offer, he climbed the stairs behind her to his room.

David's revelations about his marriage with Jo had given Sloan some insight into what had gone wrong between them, and he could see a reconciliation was possible. No matter their hardships, they shared three children together as well as mutual respect and love, even if it wasn't the glossy kind of perfection people so often expected love to be.

Was that what she wanted, to be reunited with her husband? Could she see the possibility looming? More important, was he a son of a bitch for getting in the way? He frowned as she slipped off her shoes and turned down the bed, and it struck him he hadn't been in this space with her since he was eighteen years old.

He unbuttoned his shirt, crossing to his side of the bed. In so many ways, they'd been playing house back then, pretending to be grown up when so much of who they would become was still very much in flux. But there had been a reality to it, too, a poignancy he hadn't since reclaimed. And whether it was wrong or not, he needed to do that tonight.

He unzipped his jeans, letting them fall to the floor before lifting his undershirt over his head. He hesitated. Despite what he'd told her earlier, he had not taken off his prosthesis with a woman before. It was a lie he'd told on the spur of the moment, determined to get her off the scent. But now as he stood there preparing to make love to her for the very last time, he wanted only the two of them tucked in that bed. He undid the leather strap and set the device on the floor.

She undressed facing him, first her jeans as he had done, then her sweater and bra. She sat on the edge of the bed and took off her socks before slipping between the sheets and turning toward him. He reached for her, noting the moment she realized his prosthesis was gone and bracing for her reaction.

Scooting closer to him on the bed, she kissed him tenderly on the cheek. "Thank you for everything you did today, for taking care of me and April, for welcoming David into your home." She snuggled into his side, and he stroked her back with his short fingernails.

"You know I'd do anything for you."

"You shouldn't have to. You were always taking care of me, when I should have been taking care of myself." She kissed his chest. "You made it too easy to rely on you."

He nuzzled the top of her head, the sweet smell of shampoo lingering there. "It was my pleasure."

"I should have waited for you. I shouldn't have constantly looked for someone else to solve my problems."

"You were doing the best you could. Your childhood was hard. I of all people know that."

"Maybe we all need a little more grace, a little more forgiveness."

He froze. He was nearly naked, holding on to her in his bed, yet he could feel her slipping away with the question he knew he had to ask. "Can you forgive him for what he did to you?"

"Yes. I think I can."

He squeezed his eyes shut, his arm tightening around her back, holding her to him. She lifted her knee over his leg, grazing his growing erection. It was bittersweet, the last opportunity to be with the woman who had meant so much to him, who still meant so much. He turned toward her and kissed the corner of her mouth, then her bottom lip, then her top.

She kissed him back, opening her mouth to his as she fitted herself to his body. How many times had they lain in this bed, coming together with passion and desire? A desperate need that could only be satisfied by the other, a need that could never be satisfied again.

He rolled her over, bracing himself on his arm as he

kissed the hollow between her collarbones and moved lower, kissing her heart. There could never be another woman like this one, never be another woman who owned him so completely. But this was the right thing to do, the preservation of a family that could nurture her kids, protect the life she and David had forged and allow it to grow.

He just had to have her this one last time.

His hand slid up her rib cage to cup her breast, massaging it with his fingers before taking the peak in his mouth and loving it with his tongue. She gasped, her hand moving to the back of his head to hold him against her as her body arched like a bow.

Moving lower, he followed an invisible line to her navel, then out to her hip, caressing the flesh of her leg as he made his way to the sensitive spot on the inside of her knee, kissing it and tickling it with his touch.

Her legs had fallen open to him, and he moved between them, lavishing the same attention on her other knee before making his way up the inside of her thigh. She smelled so good, and his groin flooded with heat as he opened her folds and settled on her most sensitive spot. He was determined to remember the taste of her, the sound of the little noises she made in the back of her throat as he licked and lavished her tender bud.

No woman could ever take the place of this one, no body in his bed could ever have the same grip on his heart that this woman had. And she didn't even know it. He would make love to her tonight, hold her all the while she slept, then watch as she went back to the man downstairs.

It was all he could do not to scream out loud.

He climbed up her body, his cock filling her entrance with one sure thrust. His movements were harder, his determination more intense, as if by making love to her with all his might, he could brand her as his forever.

She rolled him over and he sat up, lifting her body onto his thighs and raising her higher, both of them still intimately connected. His arm wrapped around her lower back, holding her onto him, and her breast bounced against his chin. He bent his head to catch it, latching on to her nipple and taking her deep as she did the same to his cock.

Her noises intensified, her hips thrusting faster. He needed to push her over the edge, to be the reason she came alive, and he again rolled her onto her back, driving into her center, the friction building to a fevered pitch.

He opened his eyes to see her flushed cheeks, her lashes resting against her skin, and her lips parted as she moaned. He took her mouth in a searing kiss, connecting their experience. Her muscles gripped him rhythmically, tormenting him. They milked his shaft and he was lost, his orgasm rising up like a tsunami from the calm of the sea. She cried out as his body exploded into hers, his climax ripping through him with intense pulsing waves of sensation.

He collapsed on top of her, unable to move as aftershocks ripped through his entire body, and her nails dug into his ass. The haze was slow to clear, their grip on each other lingering for long minutes as she held him inside her.

He'd never have this again.

The unfairness was an emotional blow, draining him just as her body was draining his. He rolled onto his side, taking her with him, the sound of their breath mingling on the clammy air surrounding their bodies.

He promised himself he would never forget a single detail of this night. Not her body, not her touch, not the way she made him feel, no matter who she was married to or what the future held.

28

———

Mac O'Brady stood in Sloan Dvorak's kitchen and helped himself to coffee, the light of a cloudy winter's day coming through the window. Sloan sat at the big barn-wood table with David Regan, Joanne, and Razorback. Mac had arrived at the house nearly an hour before and had yet to get a good read on the situation.

Not the passport shit with McKenzie. That was simple enough. But there was some relationship crap going down at that table, and he couldn't make hide nor hair of it. Near as he could figure, somebody was fucking somebody else, but something was seriously fucked up.

"I suggest we set a trap," he said. "If she wants the passport badly enough, she'll take the bait. We can grab her and put an end to this game of cat and mouse."

Regan straightened in his seat. "I'll do it. Confront her, tell her I'm alive, but I just want her gone. I can offer to bring the passport to her."

Sloan shook his head. "She tried to have you killed. She's

going to smell a rat a mile away. You could just as easily turn her in to the police, and she's going to suspect it."

"Then what do you suggest?" David asked. His voice held a petulant tone Mac didn't like, and he hoped Sloan would beat out that dickhead to get himself the girl.

Dvorak deserved something good in his life. A woman to share it with was the best you could hope for.

He thought of his own missing wife and the DNA results he'd received the other day. He'd become convinced a serial killer at Riker's Island might have murdered his Ellie, because she'd last been heard from when she was living in the same area at the same time as the killings, and she fit the killer's type.

He had gone to great personal and emotional expense to find the location of the graves, but while his wife wasn't among the victims, her first cousin was.

He didn't have a name, but DNA didn't lie.

Ellie had lost someone close to her at the hand of that man, and he needed to head back down south to find more information, just as soon as he helped Dvorak take care of this mess.

He gestured to Joanne with his chin. "She should do it."

"Absolutely not." Sloan stood up and headed for Mac, walking behind him for coffee. "It's dangerous. We have no idea what this woman is capable of or who she'll have gunning for her side. Her husband was connected to the Mafia, for God's sake."

Mac blew on the hot coffee. "Ain't nobody else here can do it."

"I'll do it," said Sloan.

"You just gonna drive up to that warehouse in that Porsche and yell, 'Passports! Passports for sale! Fifty cents a pass!" He chuckled at his own joke, a line from a children's book his girls used to like.

Sloan put a hand on his hip and gave Mac the stink eye. "She's desperate. She needs that passport to get the money. Without it, she's sunk. The grim reaper could dangle it off the end of a stick like a carrot, and she'd still try to reach it."

"Then I can do it," David said again.

"No," Sloan barked.

Mac shook his head. "Why not? The man has a connection to McKenzie. Whether she suspects something or not, you just said yourself she'd square dance with the devil if it meant getting that passport."

Sloan held up a hand. "It's too dangerous."

"Then you send in Joanne." Mac shrugged.

"That's an unacceptable risk." Sloan ran his hand through his hair.

"We'll be there in spades," said Mac, truly not understanding and thinking this had something to do with the fucking mess at that table. "We'll pull out all the stops. Nobody's going to get past us and hurt her."

Sloan's phone vibrated on the table. "It's my mother. We need to let the kids come back here soon." He eyed Regan, the look an indecipherable mix of anger and trust.

Mac was seriously fucking confused. "The kids know you're alive?" he asked Regan.

"Nope. And I don't want them to know until this is all over."

The phone continued to vibrate. "Then where do you suggest we put them?" Sloan asked. "You talking and breathing at my table might be a giveaway."

"So hold them off for a while," said Regan. "Send them to Chuck E. Cheese, I don't care. I'll call McKenzie and have her meet me at the warehouse." He pulled out his phone.

Sloan yanked it from his hand. "No."

Joanne let out an exasperated sigh. "Why not? Why can't he go? It's him or me, and frankly he has a history with McKenzie. We might be better off."

Mac sipped his coffee, watching the scene play out in front of him. It was time for more details. "Dvorak, I need to talk to you privately." Sloan led the way to a room with bookcases, a fireplace, and a desk. "What the fuck is going on in there, man? Let Regan be the bait."

"I can't. This woman and her associates could pack a lot of firepower. He could be killed."

"Not likely with us on the ground, but what do you care? He made his bed. Why can't he lie in it?"

"Because Joanne's still in love with him, that's why. He's the father of her children."

"Ahh." He propped his hip on the desk while Sloan paced. "And you don't want to kill off your best girl's husband, is that it?"

"Something like that."

Mac sipped from his mug. "This coffee tastes like shit."

"I'll go. Hell, David can make the call and lure her there, but I can be the bait."

"I thought you wanted Jo for yourself."

"That's not how this is going to go."

"Because...?"

"I told you. She's in love with him."

"My radar must be way off, 'cause it seemed to me like she's been sleeping with you."

Sloan shot him a warning look. Mac grinned. "I should get prizes for figuring this stuff out. Giant stuffed animals and shit."

"It doesn't matter. She and I aren't meant to be. She

thought she lost him once already. I don't want to be the reason she loses him for real."

"What if she'd prefer a one-armed, arrogant little beef-cake like you?"

"She doesn't."

"You never won a lot of stuffed animals at the fair, did you?"

"What the fuck does that mean, Mac? You're talking in goddamn riddles."

"She loves you, dumb ass."

"Maybe once. Not anymore."

"Jesus Christ. I can't deal with this shit. You've got a skull thicker than a rock." He headed for the door, turning back to point at his friend. "Regan's going in. These are my men. This is my choice. And if you think that woman's still in love with that skinny-dick little prick, you've got another think coming."

29

David set up the meeting for six o'clock so they could approach under the cover of darkness. The men of HERO Force would go first.

Sloan sat shotgun, covering his face with camo war paint. A wintery mix of ice and snow covered the roadways, making them slick, the SUV sliding through a turn before grabbing the pavement. "Glad I'm not driving the Porsche in this crap," said Mac.

HERO Force would park in a residential neighborhood on the waterfront a quarter mile from the warehouse, then make their approach on foot through a wooded area. David would drive his Porsche to the door.

David would be unarmed, despite his objections and desire for a weapon. He wasn't a trained soldier, and with six men from HERO Force running around in the dark, David would pose more of a risk than simply defending him.

There were few choices for a sniper's nest. Champion would set up on the roof of a hotel several doors down, but his view would be limited to the main entrance of the warehouse and a portion of the parking lot.

Getting into the building would be hard. There were the dual entrances from the office, where McKenzie was likely to be, a fire door at either corner of the building behind a dumpster, and one at the top of a fire escape that Sloan suspected led to the catwalk he'd observed on their earlier visit.

Biggest question was, who would be waiting for them when they got there? Sloan couldn't imagine McKenzie had any intention of letting David live. Not after what he knew and what he'd done to her cousin. There were sure to be tangos. That much was clear.

Mac parked the SUV and the men filed out. Razorback, Chop, Asher, Gavin, and Sloan. They took off at a jog through the woods, their course predetermined and understood. Sloan's mind wandered to Joanne, who'd stayed back at the house to greet the children and Evelyn. If David made it out of here alive, he would reunite with his family there tonight.

Mac's earlier words swam in his head. Did Joanne really love him? Would she choose him over David, given the choice? She'd obviously forgiven him and wanted him in her life. That didn't bode well for his chances, no matter what Mac thought.

He forced his attention to the matter at hand as the warehouse came into view in the distance. The Walkway Over the Hudson gleamed in the night sky, its light blurred and hazy from the falling ice and snow. Each man had a different plan of attack. Sloan's target was the fire escape entrance, and he was prepared to do what was necessary to breach it with explosives, a hack saw, bolt cutters, a blow torch, and lock-picking tools in his pack. He also made sure each of his teammates was prepared with pepper spray in case the dog returned.

"You see anything, Champion?" Razorback asked in their ears.

"Not a thing, gentlemen."

They reached the building, separating and heading to their individual targets. Sloan reached the fire escape, its ladder some twelve feet in the air and completely out of reach. He pulled a rope and grappling hook from his pack, swinging the metal end to catch on the ladder of the fire escape, and waited for the train to come by. According to the Metro North schedule, one should be along in the next three minutes or so.

He put his back against the wall and took in his surroundings. A small car headed down the road toward the warehouse. David was right on time. A train whistle pierced the quiet evening, the lights of the engine illuminating the ice in the air as the locomotive approached the warehouse.

As soon as the train reached him, Sloan pulled hard on the grappling hook, sending the fire escape ladder squealing to the ground. It landed with a thud, the roar of the train easily surpassing its volume, and he tucked the hook back into his pack as he quickly climbed the ladder.

David was to stay in his car until the train passed, then immediately head for the entrance. Each man of HERO Force should then be in place, provided they didn't need their explosives.

Sloan reached the top, grabbed his night vision goggles and infrared flashlight, using the combination to check out the locking mechanism on the door without calling attention to himself from the ground.

"I just need to cut a chain," said Razorback over the comm set.

"Same here," said Chop.

A heavy deadbolt could be seen through the crack in the

fire escape door, and Sloan cursed under his breath. "I need the C4."

Champion announced, "Regan's on the move. Approaching the front door from the parking lot."

Sloan rushed to set the charges, using only a small amount of the malleable explosive. He was highly aware of the age of the brick building and the possibility of additional destruction.

"Regan's reached the door."

Sloan set the detonators and quickly descended the fire escape, announcing, "Detonation in five, four, three, two, one." He jumped for the ground as he set off the charges. There was no train that could disguise the noise of an explosion. He scrambled back up the ladder the instant he hit the ground.

He could hear the other men talking as they breached the interior of the warehouse. "Tango, nine o'clock!" "Tango, six o'clock!" Gunshots rang out as Sloan reached his entrance, donned his NVGs, and drew his weapon.

Inside was eerily quiet, the catwalk before him going in two different directions, smoke and debris filling the air from the explosion. He went left, the guardrails of the catwalk only a foot or two high, and trained his weapon on the ground. He panned the area for tangos and his own men. Where the hell was everyone?

More shots rang out, movement below as someone ran between two of the tall storage racks. Sloan hurried along the catwalk to get a better view, finally catching sight of one of his own men lying prone on the floor, his weapon at the ready.

Razorback's voice came over the comm set. "Three tangos down, at least one more on the loose."

"Where's David?" asked Sloan.

"In the office."

"We got eyes?"

"Negative."

Shit. He had to get down there. Suddenly, the catwalk shook beneath his feet, and he turned to see a figure in black coming toward him just as the man fired his weapon.

Sloan returned fire, his automatic rifle firing off a dozen rounds in the time it took the tango to fire one. The figure listed sideways, then fell over the guardrail, his torso bouncing off one of the massive shelves before hitting the ground. The shelf wobbled precariously.

Turning, he ran back in the opposite direction. He needed to get to the office without being seen, and he had an idea to accomplish that. After pulling his grappling hook from his pack, he attached it to the catwalk and rappelled down the brick wall, shots ringing out and striking the brick beside him.

He reached the ground and took cover behind the same shelf as his teammate. It looked like Chop. "I'm heading for the office. Cover me," Sloan said.

"Roger."

Sloan ran to the office door, shots ringing out as Chop distracted the tangos. He reached the door and kicked it open.

David lay on the floor in a pool of blood, lifeless. Sloan barely had time to register that fact as more shots were fired. He dropped a smoke grenade and hid behind the thick metal door, bullets lodging themselves in its surface before the shooting stopped.

His night vision goggles could see through the smoke, revealing two tangos, and he shot them both long before the air cleared. "David's down. Call an ambulance. Office is clear." He crossed to the people on the floor, one female, one male, and checked them for a pulse.

Negative.

He turned to look at David, afraid to check for the same.

"Warehouse is clear!" called Razorback. "We're coming into the office." The door opened, Razorback and Chop moving to either side of David's body. "Let's get him out of here."

Sloan followed them out the door, peeling off his goggles and filling his lungs with fresh air. He bent at the waist, putting his hands on his knees. "Don't be dead, you little fucker." He spit on the ground and closed his eyes. "Just don't be dead."

30

———

The bright lights of the emergency department belied the fatigue in Joanne's bones. She hugged herself tightly as she finished recounting the events of the last several days to the plainclothes detective who'd investigated David's death. "And then I got the call and came here."

"Is he going to make it?"

She frowned. "We don't know yet. He's still in surgery."

He folded up his small notepad and tucked it into the pocket of his jacket. "Mrs. Regan, I owe you an apology. I don't think I made a secret of the fact that I believed you were somehow responsible for your husband's death."

"Thank you. I appreciate that."

"You do realize that, if he survives, he'll have to face charges for the death of McKenzie Bannon's cousin, Finbar."

"I know he will, but I believe it was in self-defense."

"I'm going to take your word on that one for now. If it comes down to an investigation, we'll have to see what comes to light, but I'd say your family has been through enough for one week."

That was the understatement of the century, and she couldn't help but laugh. "I agree."

The detective left her his business card and promised to return in the morning to check on David. She tucked it in her purse and walked down the long hall, recounting what David had said about fatherhood and how difficult it had been to break the chain of bad parenting they'd both been caught up in.

Please give him another chance.

Let him be a father to his children.

Help him learn and grow.

While their marriage wasn't something she cared to fix, he would always belong to Fiona, Lucas, and April. She could help him embrace that role. Be a friend to him when he needed it most.

She would like that.

To think, a week ago she was planning a funeral he would have hated, purely out of spite. She wasn't proud of herself for that, and she swore, if David lived, she would find a way to get along better with him, if only for the kids' sake.

She curled up on a comfortable chair, letting her leg dangle over one side. Where was Sloan? Mac had been here earlier to check on her, and Evelyn had called. But Sloan was notably missing, and she was oddly hurt by his absence.

Whereas she knew what she wanted from David, she had no such understanding about Sloan. She knew she loved him. She had always loved him. But did he want to be with her?

She wasn't the same person she'd been then. She was a grown woman with a family and responsibilities he might not want to share, especially with David tucked awkwardly in the picture.

Baggage. She came with a lot of baggage, and she

needed to learn to stand on her own two feet. She bit her nail, staring into space as time stretched indefinitely.

"Jo."

She turned at her name, finding Sloan standing in front of her, showered and clean with his good arm in a sling. "What happened?" she asked.

"No big deal. Just a little scrape."

"You needed a sling for a scrape?"

"A little bullet scrape."

She huffed. "Then why would you say it was only a scrape?"

"Because I didn't want you to worry." He sat down in the chair next to her. "How is he doing?" His voice cracked.

"Still in surgery."

"Is he going to make it?"

The emotions she'd been holding inside suddenly rose up to the surface. Her eyes burned. "I don't know. He's been in there a long time."

He held out his prosthetic arm and she leaned into it, but the material was cold and the contact awkward. She pulled away. "Can you keep a secret?"

"Sure."

"At his funeral, I was glad he was dead." She wiped at her eyes with the heels of her hands. "How awful is that? I was bitter and so full of hate. Now I'm sitting here praying he lives."

"You can't blame yourself."

"Can't I?" She shook her head. "We were married more than a dozen years, and I couldn't see his side enough to even care if he was alive. I'm ashamed of those feelings now. I don't know what I'm going to do if he doesn't pull through. The kids need him. I need him."

A tall woman in blue scrubs and a cap pushed through

the double doors that led to the surgery department. "Mrs. Regan?"

She stood and stepped forward, away from Sloan. "Yes."

"I'm Dr. Winslow. I operated on your husband. He had two bullet wounds. Each bullet passed completely through his upper torso." She sighed heavily, then smiled. "He's a very lucky man. He'll be in recovery for an hour or two, but then you can see him."

She instantly began sobbing, happy tears filling her eyes and spilling onto her cheeks. "He's going to be all right?"

"Yes, he is."

She hugged the doctor with all her might. "Oh, thank you! Thank you so much for taking such good care of him." She turned to Sloan. "Isn't that gr—"

She could just see him at the far end of the hall, the strap from his sling standing out from his dark shirt as he pushed through a swinging door. "Isn't that great?" she whispered, but Sloan was gone.

31

Trace belched. "Give me four."

Mac clucked his tongue. "There's a two-card limit, Langston. Just like last hand."

"Then fuck. Give me two."

Sloan put his cards facedown. "I fold."

"What the hell, Dvorak?" asked Trace. "You gonna play or not?"

"Not." He moved to the kitchen and grabbed a bag of Cheetos, opening them and throwing them into the middle of the table.

Mac raised an eyebrow at him. "What happened to the filet mignon?"

"I'm fresh out."

"I'll take one," said Moto.

"Dealer takes two," said Mac.

Poker was a terrible idea. What was he thinking inviting them over here tonight? He'd been in a foul mood for the past two weeks, and company wasn't improving it one damn bit.

He knew what his problem was. He missed Jo. He was being the grown-up, doing the right thing, and giving her and David some space to work things out. But he hated it, every brain cell he had left screaming for him to do the wrong thing, be the bad guy, and go get the girl.

"I'm going to be taking a leave of absence from work," said Mac, throwing two chips into the pot. "I have some personal business I need to take care of."

Sloan sat back down. "Everything all right?"

"Yep, just looking for my Ellie is all." Mac looked to Trace. "You in?"

"I'll raise you twenty." He burped again. "Jesus, this Mexican beer is killing me. Who's going to be in charge while you're away?"

"I figured Sloan here can do it."

Sloan scowled. "Why me?"

"You decided to stay with HERO Force, ain't that right? Figure you should try on management for size."

He'd been continuing to weigh his options since Joanne left. Helping her had made him feel useful again, valuable. Like maybe he had something to contribute to the team, after all. If he hadn't worked for HERO Force, he never would have been able to help. Still, he resented Mac's assumption. "I never said for sure."

"Ah, but you meant to. Just slipped your mind. You try sitting behind the big desk for a while, calling the shots. Let me know how you like it when I get back."

"Fine."

The doorbell rang and Gus headed for it, barking his head off. Sloan grabbed a handful of Cheetos and went to answer it, freezing when the dog's barks changed to a plaintive whine. He cocked his head, hope rising up in his chest. "Who is it, boy?"

He got close enough to hear Fiona's gravelly voice from the other side. "Hello, puppy, puppy, puppy..."

A smile spread across his face as he opened the door. "Surprise!" yelled Fiona and Lucas. April waved. Joanne stood in the back, her expression more difficult to read.

He opened the storm door, the dog rushing past to leap on Joanne. "Come on in."

Fiona hugged his legs and he bent down to hug her properly. Lucas also came in for a hug, though he patted Sloan's back like a man hugging a man. April scooted by with another wave. "Hi, Sloan." Until only Jo and Gus were left on the porch.

"Hi, there," she said, her cheeks filling with color and her eyes sparkling. Hope sprang to life for the first time in weeks.

He stepped outside.

He should ask her why she was here.

He should ask her how David was doing.

I should hold her tight and never let her go.

"Look out, dog." He lightly pushed Gus out of the way, took Jo in his arms, and kissed her.

She chuckled. "You taste like Cheese-its."

"Cheetos. Come here, you sexy thing." He turned her around and pressed her against the house, kissing her thoroughly. "Tell me you're not going back to David."

"I'm not going back to David."

"Tell me you're coming back to stay."

She pulled back and laughed. "I was just going to ask you to dinner."

"Oh, we're way past dinner, honey." He kissed her more deeply, letting his fingers trace the side of her face. "I don't ever want to be without you again. Besides, my dog really likes you."

She rested her forehead against his and sighed. "He's our dog, you jerk. Now let's go inside."

EPILOGUE

Fiona's eyes went wide and her mouth dropped into an O. She took the pink and purple apron from Sloan. "I get princesses?"

"You sure do, sweetheart. You're going to be in charge of the powdered sugar."

She hugged it to herself and spun from side to side. "Thank you, thank you, thank you!"

He moved to Lucas, who'd already put on his NASCAR apron. "Hold it like this, then drizzle the honey out in a thin, swooshy line." He demonstrated on a paper plate. "Give it a practice try."

"I think the oil's hot enough," said April, whose bright yellow apron had a more adult, geometric motif. "It's wavy, like you said."

"Okay, flatten the dough into a circle with the heel of your hand, like this." She did as he demonstrated. "Perfect. Now take the tongs and gently place it in the oil. Try not to drop it, or it will splatter."

Joanne walked into the kitchen. "It smells amazing in here."

"I got princesses!" yelled Fiona. "And I do the sugar."

"I'm sure you'll do a wonderful job." She crossed to Sloan and slipped her hand around his waist. "David's going to be here in about twenty minutes to pick up the kids."

"Where's he taking us?" asked Lucas.

"Laser golf and the batting cages at the mall, then you're sleeping at his new apartment." All three kids turned to stare at their mom. "He has enough room now. He wants you to stay."

"Yay!" said Fiona. "We're sleeping at Daddy's today. Can I bring my princess dress?"

"The apron?" asked Sloan. "Why not." He checked on April's fried dough. "See how the edges are turning golden brown? You can flip it over now. Just be careful."

When the dough was done, Lucas covered it in a thin swirl of honey and Fiona dusted it with an inch of powdered sugar. "Oops, sorry." She stuck out her bottom lip.

"Looks good to me," said Sloan, tearing off a piece and popping it in his mouth. "So delicious."

Everyone tore off a piece and proclaimed it to be the the best fried dough any of them had ever eaten. "I'll finish this up," said Sloan. "You guys get cleaned up for your dad."

Joanne ran her finger through the powdered sugar on the countertop. "It's amazing how much of a mess they can make in such a short period of time. What do you want to do tonight?"

"I don't care, as long as we're naked."

She wrapped her arms around his neck. "It's like you can read my mind." She kissed him. "You taste like powdered sugar."

He wagged his eyebrows. "I have some honey in a squeeze bottle we can probably find a use for."

"Sounds messy."

He kissed her, pinning her hips against the counter. "Don't worry, miss, I'm a professional."

THANK you for reading Holding his Hostage. If you enjoyed this book, you'll love Engaging his Enemy. Get it now, or keep reading for an excerpt.

BOOKS BY AMY GAMET

Click here to see all books on Amazon

Box sets also available

HERO Force

1. Stranded with the SEAL (Hawk & Olivia)

2. Sheltered by the SEAL (Jax & Jessa)

3. Harbored by the SEAL (Cowboy & Charlotte)

4. Married to the SEAL (Matteo & Grace)

5. Justice for the SEAL (Logan & Gemma)

6. Targeted by the SEAL (Austin & Cassidy)

7. Kidnapped by the SEAL (Noah & Hannah)

8. Forever with the SEAL (Hawk & Olivia wedding)

Shattered SEALs (HERO Force New York)

1. Protecting his Witness (Luke & Summer)

2. Resisting his Target (Razorback & Jackie)

3. Holding his Hostage (Sloan & Joanne)

4. Engaging his Enemy (Zack & Davina)

5. Fighting his Fate (Brett & Grace)

6. Reclaiming his Honor (Mac & Ellie)

Love on the Lake (contemporary romance)

1. Treasure on Moon Lake (Gabe & Tori)

2. Fortune on Moon Lake (Rafael & Melanie)

ENGAGING HIS ENEMY CHAPTER 1

Zach "Moto" Sato wiped sweat from his brow, hot on the trail of a kidnapper. Four thousand miles away, a teenage girl's life hung in the balance, a series of keystrokes here in New York HERO Force's only hope to find her.

This was what he was good at, his skills honed like the tip of a bowman's arrow. He could wield a firearm as surely as his SEAL team brethren, but computers were his weapon of choice, the system of interconnected machines and languages the currency with which he would secure the girl's freedom.

This job was a dream come true, a chance to go after the devil himself on his own terms. It was as if he'd spent his life preparing for this job, his education and military training converging on his position at HERO Force like a laser. Somewhere out there, the girl's desperate parents waited for her return, and Moto was hell-bent the men who'd taken her would pay the price for their actions.

The door behind him opened and a deep voice belched. "There's pizza in the conference room," said Trace.

"I'm a little busy here."

"They make the drop?"

"Late last night." Moto had been at his computer ever since.

"And the girl?"

"Not yet. Supposed to be returned by sundown."

"Tell me you got the bastards."

"Almost." The ransom had been paid in electronic currency, as demanded by the kidnappers, and immediately disappeared into an internet labyrinth hidden behind fire-walls and state-of-the-art encryption. Ninety-nine out of a hundred computer programmers would have lost the trail right out of the gate. Of the one percent capable of tracking it, Moto knew he was one of the best.

It wasn't arrogance, it was confidence and an accurate understanding of his abilities. God willing, the girl would be returned safe and sound. But if not, or hell, even if she was, their only chance of finding the people responsible for her ordeal and getting any kind of justice lay in his hands. "I tracked the funds to an account in Liechtenstein, where they split up into hundreds of individual packets, each routed to a different destination."

"How the fuck do you track 'em all?"

"I don't. I make the computer do it. I created a virus that investigates each individual transaction routed out of the account in Liechtenstein. A little bit of code that follows each electronic signature and reports back to me. All those packets need to converge again at their final destination, which means my code will recognize itself and tell me where the money went."

"You can do that?"

"I can."

"Is it legal?"

Moto narrowed his eyes. "Kidnapping is illegal."

Trace took a swig of Mountain Dew, then raised it in a mock toast. "I'm good with that logic."

Moto considered Trace a friend, a position only a few of his teammates occupied. He respected the others, had put his life in their hands on several occasions, but true friendship was a matter of another kind. His trust was hard-won and unable to be restored when broken. Moto trusted Trace.

Mac walked into the room. The leader of HERO Force had stayed the night at the office, just as Moto had, the older man's youthful gait belying any fatigue. "Moto, you've got a phone call on line two. It wouldn't ring through for some reason."

"I put it on do not disturb."

Mac clicked it off. "Someone named Davina."

Moto's head snapped up. He hadn't heard that name since he'd left home ten years earlier, and the very sound of it made the wall he'd built around the past vibrate and shake. He refocused on his computer screen. "Take a message. I can't talk to her now."

"She says it's important."

He hesitated, his mind instantly flashing to his brother with a painful lurch. Was Ben okay? He wouldn't have thought he could be so affected by the thought of his brother hurt or in need. Memory was funny like that, refusing to bow to distance or apathy. He set his jaw. "This is more important."

Trace perched his hip on the opposite side of Moto's desk. "Davina, huh? Nice name. She pretty?"

Moto glared at him, even as her image floated up from his mind. He'd once thought her more beautiful than any woman could be, but betrayal had a way of turning even the sweetest features foul. "No."

"That the chick from the party last week?"

A petite brunette with a low-cut blouse and a particularly small vocabulary. Moto had thrown away her number. "No."

"Tinder?"

He'd never even downloaded the app. "God no."

Mac gestured to the phone. "So, why don't you answer it?"

"I'm working."

Trace frowned. "Is there a whole lot you can do until those packets arrive at the end of the line?"

"I'm monitoring the process. Making sure the tracing virus is doing its job. Tell her I'll call her back."

Mac picked up the phone on Moto's desk. "He'll have to call you back." He listened for a moment, then put the handset on his chest. "She says it's an emergency."

Moto hesitated. That phone was a connection to his past and the people he'd left behind, and he wasn't so keen on accepting it. But what if something was wrong? What if Ben had been hurt or needed a kidney?

That fucker's not getting one of my kidneys.

His hand reached out for the phone as if in slow motion. What if Ben was dead, the rift between them cementing like some kind of cosmic stone, unable to be rewritten? A twinge of regret pierced his consciousness. "Hello?"

"Zach, I need your help." Her voice cut a slice down deep into bone. No one had called him by his given name in years, the sound of it like an echo he hadn't expected. But it was the concern in her voice that alarmed him. "What's wrong?"

"Ben's been arrested."

Moto squeezed his eyes shut and bowed his head. Anger with his brother and this woman was instantaneous. He shouldn't have gotten on the phone. "This is why you called?"

"Please. They think he killed a federal agent."

"Murder?" That got his attention. Ben had always been looking for the easy way out, a shortcut designed to thwart hard work and provide the greatest reward with the least amount of effort, but murder? He squeezed the skin between his eyes. Who knew what time and desperation could do to a man?

"He needs your help," she pleaded.

She sounded so concerned for her husband. Were the two of them still together after all this time? Had the young girl who'd stolen his heart and then gutted him with her betrayal been living this whole time with his brother, sharing Ben's bed? The idea hurt like alcohol on a wound, bitterness like a storm over a raging sea. "What he needs is a lawyer. What are you calling me for?"

"He has a lawyer. He was set up, Zach. He's being framed."

Moto rolled his eyes. Someone else was always responsible for Ben's problems, no matter how big or how small. "Of course he is."

"He is! And he says you're the only one good enough to help him, that somebody created all this fake evidence on his computer."

"Look, there's nothing I can do to help him. If there's a trail of evidence, it's probably because he did it." His eyes went to the computer screen as the machine spit out a string of IP addresses and electronic routing numbers. The packets he'd been tracking had arrived at their final destination. "I have to go."

"Please, he needs you," she begged. "It's all this computer stuff, and his lawyer says they have an open-and-shut case, but it's all fake evidence. You have to help us."

Us.

The pronoun scratched at his insides like he'd swallowed a beast. No way would he go back there. No way would he let them in. Ben didn't need his help. Yes, Moto's skills were some of the best in the world, but it was highly unlikely such a detailed knowledge of forensic computing was necessary. "Someone else will have to help him. I'm sorry."

"He needs you. No matter how you feel about me, you have to know how hard it was for him to reach out like this. How can you just leave him in his hour of need?"

"Oh, that's rich, coming from you."

"Damn it, Zach, come home."

"I am home, Davina." He hung up the phone, aware of the curious eyes of the other men as he worked. He homed in on the guilty account, printing out a name and account number before locating their tango in the national database of scumbags. His heart was racing, the kidnapper in his sights having nothing to do with the adrenaline overwhelming his system. "John Patrick Kilbourne, age thirty-nine. An Armenian national with a hell of a rap sheet and a very public bone to pick."

He handed the printouts to Mac.

"Good work. You trace all the money?"

"Every last dime."

The intercom on the phone buzzed. "Moto, you've got a call on line one."

His head dropped to his chest and he forced himself to breathe. "Take a message."

"She says it's an emergency."

"Jesus Christ," he grumbled under his breath, punching the blinking light and answering the phone. "Damn it, Davina—"

"Shut up and listen," she snapped. "I promised myself I wasn't going to do this. I swore to God in heaven I wouldn't give you the freaking satisfaction of stooping to this level, but your incredibly selfish attitude leaves me no choice. If you can't find it in your heart to help Ben, if you truly hate your *own brother* so much because of some stupid misunderstanding that happened years ago, then come back for your son."

"*What?*"

"You heard me."

"But Ben—"

"No, Zach. Wyatt is *your* son. At the very least, you owe it to him to meet him face-to-face. Just don't stay too long or else he'll figure out what an egotistical, self-centered jackass you are."

The phone went dead in his hand. He took it away from his ear and stared at it. The clock ticked loudly on the wall. Davina's baby had been his child. His child, not Ben's. Sweat broke out across his body as an image appeared in his mind, a pregnant Davina in the distance, waddling down the high school steps as Ben gloated in Moto's ear. *"We're getting married."*

He hung up the phone with a trembling hand and covered his mouth with his fingers.

Mac cocked his head and eyed him questioningly. "What's up?"

"I need some time off." He swallowed against the panic that rose in his throat like bile. "All the information on the kidnappers is there. I printed it out. I gotta go."

"Where are you going?" asked Trace.

Nothing scared Moto. Not gunfire. Not a steady stream of tangos headed his way. But this was fear, sure as the blood was draining from his head and weighing down his feet like concrete in his boots. He looked from one man to the other. "I'm going home."

ENGAGING HIS ENEMY CHAPTER 2

Yea, though I walk through the valley of the shadow of death...

The world as Zach knew it was over. His parents were dead, killed in a snowy collision with a tractor trailer on their way to pick Ben up from a party where he'd had too much to drink. The horror of it was too difficult to bear, the desperate need to connect with another human being too much for Zach to control.

The funeral ended just hours before. Davina was fitted beneath him on his bed, her skirt around her waist, the sweet heat of her groin through her cotton panties and the gentle touch of her fingernails across his fevered skin tempting him to steamroll over the line he'd sworn never to cross.

She was sixteen to his eighteen, a year and a half into a relationship her parents had never wanted to be—for this very reason. And he'd tried, oh, how he'd tried to resist her, but the pain of loss was raw and demanding a desperate response, an act of love to fill him up where grief had drained him completely.

Her hand slipped beneath his shirt and skated over his lower back, then lower, cupping his ass through his dress slacks. His hips jerked forward in response, the sensation of his eager erection against her willing body almost too much to bear, even through their clothes. He looked into her eyes. "We have to stop." He didn't even have a condom.

"I love you." It wasn't the first time she'd said the words, but this time they meant something different. She wanted to make love with him. Or was she only saying that to offer comfort in his time of need?

I shall fear no evil. Thy rod and thy staff they comfort me...

Images from the last few days assaulted him, the pain of grief threatening to drown him before he took her mouth in a desperate kiss that instantly chased the darkness away. More than a year he'd wanted her like this, hundreds of days of careful control insisting he force his hands to his sides even as he longed to stroke her tender flesh.

She unbuttoned his dress shirt, those nails scraping his chest as she went. He wasn't capable of stopping, hadn't the will or the desire to push away the one person he needed now more than he'd ever needed anyone.

She moved to her own shirt, unbuttoning her blouse, exposing a plain white bra with a satin bow in the middle, her breasts burgeoning from the top of the garment as if she'd outgrown it long ago. He buried his face in her cleavage, inhaling the scent of her heated skin and all she was offering.

His hand reached up to cup her breast, and her breath caught in her throat with a tiny moan of longing. "Jesus Christ," he whispered reverently, wrapping his arms around her to undo the clasp of her bra and exposing her completely to his hungry stare. Her nipples were dark, the tips protruding like glorious peaks from perfectly shaped mounds, and his lips went to them of their own accord, tasting her with his tongue before sucking her fullness into the depths of his mouth.

Her back arched and her legs trembled. There was no going back. The hardness of her nipple against the roof of his mouth felt like it was meant to be there, his tongue and jaw knowing how to caress her without ever having been told. She writhed beneath him, her hips insistent against his as her breath came in little spurts and gasps.

Moving higher, he kissed along her neck until he was eye to eye with her. His cock was so engorged, even the friction of the change in position was threatening his control. He'd never been with a woman, having long since decided to wait for this one. "Are you sure?"

She nodded. Bracing his weight on his elbow, he reached down with his other hand and undid his belt. She held up a hand. "Wait." Disappointment crested over him, but he worked to keep his expression the same as she struggled to sit up and turned back to look at him. "Lie on your back," she whispered.

She wasn't going anywhere.

He did as she asked, aware of the hard ridge of his penis tenting his pants as her stare moved down to see it. Then her hands were on him, carefully unzipping his fly and releasing his erection. He thought again of his need for a condom and wondered if his brother might have one he could use. But he was angry with Ben for the role he'd played in his parents' death and was equally sure Ben would try to talk him out of making love to Davina.

He would pull out. His cock twitched with eager desperation, the thought of being inside her driving him insane as she lightly grazed his length before fisting her fingers around the base of his shaft and squeezing him tightly. He cursed under his breath and she quickly let him go. She suddenly looked scared.

He touched her arm. "We don't have to do this."

"Is it going to hurt?"

"I don't know."

She nodded, reaching for his pants and pushing them down his body, then carefully removing his socks. She took off her open blouse, dropping it to the floor, then the bra that dangled from her arms before moving to the waistband of her skirt.

"I want to do it." His voice was a growl, barely recognizable to his own ears. He wanted to undress her, needed to be the first man to take off the garments that hid her from view. His hands slipped beneath the fabric to cup her bare hips, taking her skirt and panties down in one movement, caressing her thighs and calves. His face was close to her mound, and he sniffed the heavily perfumed air at the apex of her thighs, his erection bouncing with his need to have her.

Davina was perfect, every curve of her body, the satiny feel of her skin, the way she pulled him on top of her despite her obvious fear. He needed to get lost in her, but he also needed this to be good for her, his inexperience telling him only to go as slowly as he could muster. He kissed her lips reverently, and she opened to him, taking him in her mouth as the head of his swollen cock pressed at the entrance to her body.

She was slick, and the first inch or two slipped inside with ease, the sensation of her enveloping heat better than any he'd ever known. But she tensed up beneath him, and he instinctively retreated, drawing his attention back to her mouth, her breasts, her waist as she once again pressed her hips against him. Gripping the base of his cock, he guided himself back into her tight channel. This time, she didn't resist when he pressed farther inside.

He gasped with pleasure, desperate to thrust himself fully into her body. He lifted his head, his stare melding with hers in complete understanding. She wanted him no matter what that meant, be it pleasure or pain, fear or reckless abandon. He withdrew and thrust deeper into her core, pressing against a barrier that prevented further passage.

Bracing her shoulders with his arm, he kissed her neck and whispered in her ear, "I love you." With one hard thrust, he broke through the barrier and filled her completely, her body clenching in obvious pain. "I'm sorry. I'm sorry. Shhh…" he coddled.

Slowly she relaxed beneath him, though he dared not move. Her arms came around him and she held him tightly. "I love you, too."

He lifted his head and she kissed him, her hands moving up and into his hair as her hips began to move. The sensation was at once overwhelming, his release already on the horizon as he met her movements with his own. She wrapped her legs tightly around his waist, her cheeks flushing a deep crimson. "You feel good."

He needed to pull out before he came inside her, but making love to this woman was more powerful than his will to stop. He needed to stay with her, to be buried as deeply in her body as he could to chase the demons away that waited to choke him the moment he stopped.

He pumped harder, faster, deeper. With one final thrust, the world exploded in a rush of sensation and color, his climax ripping a feral growl from deep in his abdomen as he emptied himself into the woman he loved.

How could he have known she would betray him less than a week later?

A flight attendant stopped beside him, snapping his attention back to the present. "Would you care for a drink, sir?"

He felt an intense craving for something alcoholic and strong. "Water."

She smiled the bright smile of a woman more interested in getting his number than serving him a beverage, and he turned away, looking out the window. They were nearing the airport, a cloudless sky showing they were closer to the ground than when he'd last checked, and his jaw hardened at the thought of landing in Houston.

It didn't make any goddamn sense. If Wyatt really was his child, Davina must have known she'd been pregnant when she came to see him at basic training. Why in God's name hadn't she said something then, before she'd married his brother?

"Sir," said the flight attendant, and he took the drink, thanking her. He drank it in one chug, instantly wishing he'd gone for vodka after all.

He swirled the ice in the plastic cup. Maybe Davina hadn't known who the father was. Maybe she still didn't know, and she was fucking with him to get him to help Ben. Her husband was being charged with murder. What wife wouldn't go to great lengths to free the man she loved?

The thought pierced the armor that protected his heart. He flagged down the eager flight attendant with the slightest of waves. "Vodka, please. And make it a double." He stared back out the window. The plane was about to land smack dab in the middle of hell, and he might as well do it with a drink in his hand.

KEEP READING ENGAGING HIS ENEMY. Get it now.

ABOUT THE AUTHOR

Amy Gamet is a USA Today bestselling author who lives in upstate New York with her husband, children, too many pets and the occasional foster animal or litter. She likes to swim in the sunshine, make jewelry, and lobbies professionally for household remodeling projects. She owns an unusual number of brightly colored T-shirts and black yoga pants, and her children always ask who's coming to visit when she runs the vacuum cleaner.

www.amygamet.com